D1564629

THE DEVIL
AND THE
DETECTIVE
John Goldbach

Coach House Books, Toronto

Canada Council   Conseil des Arts   ONTARIO ARTS COUNCIL
for the Arts   du Canada   CONSEIL DES ARTS DE L'ONTARIO

Published with the generous assistance of the Canada Council for the
Arts and the Ontario Arts Council. Coach House Books also acknowl-
edges the support of the Government of Canada through the Canada
Book Fund and the Government of Ontario through the Ontario Book
Publishing Tax Credit.

LIBRARY AND ARCHIVES CANADA CATALOGUING IN PUBLICATION

Goldbach, John, 1978-
     The devil and the detective / John Goldbach.

Also issued in electronic format.
ISBN 978-1-55245-269-1

     I. Title.

PS8613.O432D49 2013   C813'.6   C2013-900218-9

The Devil and the Detective is available as an ebook:
ISBN 978 1 77056 335 3.

Purchase of the print version of this book entitles you to a free digital
copy. To claim your ebook of this title, please email sales@chbooks.com
with proof of purchase or visit chbooks.com/digital. (Coach House
Books reserves the right to terminate the free digital download offer at
any time.)

'Le grotesque des événements de tous les jours vous cache le vrai malheur des passions.'

– Antoine Barnave

'By the next day the mastermind had completely solved the mystery – with the exception of locating the pearls and finding the thief.'

– from Buster Keaton's *Sherlock Jr.*

Contents

1

Crime is law. Law is crime. That much is obvious. Interpret it however you like but it still holds.

Enough abstraction. Time for the case.

The phone call came in the late evening and the woman on the other end of the line was crying.

'Mr. James,' she said.

'Yes,' I said.

'I need your help,' she said. 'My husband. He's been murdered.'

'How did you get my number?'

'Martin Bouvert. My lawyer. He gave it to me.' She started weeping. 'Mr. James, please. I need your help. He's been stabbed in the chest. Gerald's been stabbed in the chest!'

'Calm down, ma'am. I don't even know your name.'

'Elaine,' she said. 'Elaine Andrews.'

Although it was late I was awake, or somewhat awake. I'd been reading a book on the couch and drinking whiskies. I was tired and groggy but still awake.

'Have you called the police, Mrs. Andrews? Where's your husband?'

'Yes … I've called the police … and my husband's in the living room, with a knife in his chest … He's soaked in blood … '

'When did you find him?'

'Just now, when I woke up. When I saw he wasn't in bed I called out to him and there wasn't an answer so I went to go look for him and when I found him he was downstairs in the living room, laid out on the couch, with a knife in his chest!'

'Where do you live?'

'Tower Street, 19 Tower Street. Please, come soon.'

'I will, Mrs. Andrews, but I'd like to ask you one more question … '

'Yes … '

'Why have you asked me to come so quickly? I mean, you haven't even talked to the police, or at least they haven't shown up at your home yet … So why call me immediately?'

'I called the police first, and then my lawyer, and he told me to call a private detective. He gave me your number. He said you'd be discreet.'

'Are there things we need to be discreet about?'

'He just seemed to think it was a good idea. That's the doorbell,' she said. 'Probably the police. Come soon please … '

After she hung up her phone I stood with mine still in my hand, listening to the dead line. I put the phone back on its mount and sat down on the couch and drank my drink. I wasn't sure why she was calling me, a private detective, before the police – although useless for anything other than exerting unnecessary force – even had a crack at the case. Something's fishy, I thought, without a doubt. Her lawyer was overly cautious, I thought, sitting on the couch, whisky in hand, contemplating the case. The case of Mr. Gerald Andrews. Gerald Andrews, with his wife, Elaine Andrews, and a knife in his chest. Their names were so boring, so commonplace as to seem improbable. At the very least, I thought, groggy from the drink, Mr. Gerald Andrews's death, whether caused by murder or suicide or some freak accident, would bring considerable excitement to Mrs. Elaine Andrews's life. Elaine Andrews, who is this woman? I wondered, while sitting on the couch, shortly after she called me, shortly after the expiration of her husband, Gerald Andrews. They both had old people's names, but Elaine Andrews's voice sounded young, or at least not old. Under forty, I suspected, but I'm often wrong when it comes to guessing people's ages, especially over the telephone. There are a lot of things I get wrong when it comes to guesswork. I observe, and then I come to a conclusion, if there's a conclusion to come to, which more often than not there isn't. A lot remains unknown. Things change while you look at them. I better get dressed, I thought, sitting on the couch, so I finished my drink and took a shower.

The water was hot, as always in my building, and the bathroom filled with steam. I stood in the shower, under the hot water, trying to sober up a little, thinking of Elaine Andrews. There was something strange about her voice. She sounded young, and maybe didn't sound sad, though she was crying, crying considerably, and she sounded scared. Of course she sounded scared, I thought, she'd just found her husband with a knife protruding from his chest on their chesterfield. Usually I would've thought *couch*, I thought, and wasn't that the word Mrs. Andrews, Elaine Andrews, used when she called? Didn't she say *couch, I found my husband on the* couch *with a knife in his chest*? I'm sure that's what she said, I thought, standing in the shower, in the steam-filled washroom, under extremely hot water. Her voice sounded strange. Young, quite young, under forty, but perhaps under thirty, though I wasn't sure. Perhaps her voice sounded young because she was crying. Crying tends to be something young people do, or at least hysterical crying – older people don't cry hysterically, I thought. Babies cry hysterically, of course, because they are babies and not yet resigned to this world. Teenage girls, too, cry hysterically, though older people don't, I thought, or at least that's what I'd observed over the years, the years of my life, which aren't many, when considering the history of human life, so perhaps I'm just inexperienced when it comes to the hysterical tears of old people. Old people, the ones with dementia, them I could see crying hysterically, I thought, standing in the hot water of the shower. Mrs. Andrews, however, didn't sound old; on the contrary, she sounded young – she sounded young and sexy. Why sexy? What led me to believe she was sexy? Perhaps she wasn't, though something in her voice sounded sexy. Desperation? Was desperation sexy? Usually not, I thought. When a man seems desperate, desperate to get laid, for instance, that's when it never happens, unless of course he's willing to pay, but that's different. To be fair, it's not that sexy when a woman is desperate, or overly desperate, either – but Mrs. Andrews's desperation was different. She was desperate for me to help her. She was desperate for my services. She sounded like perhaps I could help her, that perhaps I was the only one who could, and maybe that's what I found sexy. Maybe she was still in her nightgown, I thought, or maybe that's what made me think she was so sexy sounding, that is to say, the possibility that she was still in her nightgown when she called. Or a silk robe, with nothing on underneath. But the police were on their way. She'd dress for the police, I thought. But when she found the body, the dead body of her husband, after she'd called out to him from their bed in the night, she was most likely scantily clad, perhaps even totally nude. This young woman was perhaps totally nude, I thought while showering, when she found her husband laid out on the couch with a knife protruding from his chest. Or at least she was probably totally nude before finding him, when she was alone in bed. I thought about this for a few more minutes while I finished my shower.

When my cab pulled up near Mrs. Elaine Andrews's house – formerly Mr. Gerald Andrews's house, too – there were two police cars in the driveway: one a black-and-white squad car, the other a dark blue unmarked car of the same make and model. Mrs. Elaine Andrews, Elaine Andrews, Elaine, was standing on the porch, crying, dressed, wearing a tan raincoat. It looked like she was giving a uniformed officer her statement. She didn't see me right away, which was for the best. It gave me an opportunity to appraise the situation, to get a good look at the scene and observe everything before the knowledge of my presence corrupted things as they were. Elaine sniffled into a handkerchief while looking down at her shoes. The uniformed officer took notes in his notepad – something I never do till afterward – while she stood there crying; it didn't look like she was saying much. Nevertheless, he kept scribbling away, taking notes *in situ*. Perhaps, I thought, he wasn't only recording what she was saying; perhaps he was writing about what he was thinking about what she was saying, or speculating on why she wasn't saying anything when she wasn't saying anything, and when she was talking perhaps he was writing that down, too: *Why isn't she talking?*, he wrote, perhaps, I thought. *Is it because of her tears? Mr. Gerald Andrews*, he wrote, perhaps, *though unlucky to have been stabbed to death, was lucky to have been with such a sexy woman while alive* – and she was, that is to say, sexy.

There seemed to be movement in the house. The other officers, a couple of plainclothesmen, were stomping all over the crime scene. They were inside, examining the body, examining the wounds, dusting for fingerprints, and so on, I figured. I don't like that stuff. That's one of the reasons I'm a private detective. There are many reasons, actually. That's definitely one, though. I hate all that bullshit. Regardless. No one had seen me and the uniformed officer didn't seem to be getting anywhere with Elaine, so I decided it was time for me to make my presence known.

'Good evening, Mrs. Andrews,' I said, then, 'Good evening, officer.'

'Mr. James,' she said. 'I'm glad you've made it.'

'Is this a friend of yours, ma'am?' asked the officer.

'He's a private detective I've asked for assistance.'

Just then a police detective, Detective Michael O'Meara, a man I'm familiar with, came out the front door and joined us on the front porch.

'Well, well,' he said. 'Rick, to what do we owe the pleasure?'

'Mrs. Andrews called me and asked for my services.'

'You don't have faith in the police, Mrs. Andrews?'

'With all due respect, Detective O'Meara, my husband's just been murdered and I'm anxious that we get to the bottom of this as soon as possible. And, yes,' she said, like a pro, 'I have faith in the police but realize that you are underfunded and understaffed and thought that you'd appreciate all the help you can get. Besides, Mr. James has a very good reputation. Can we really say the same about the police department, Detective O'Meara?'

He stood speechless, as did the uniformed officer, who didn't write anything in his notepad, and I blushed from the compliment. O'Meara's a pain in the ass, if the truth be known, and deserved to be put in his place.

'If we're through for now, officers,' Mrs. Andrews continued, 'I'd like to talk to Mr. James in private. So if you'll please excuse us. Thank you for your help.'

'We can't leave the scene yet, Mrs. Andrews,' said O'Meara.

'Yes, though I can – can't I?'

'I don't see why not. We have your cell number.'

'Thank you, officers. Mr. James,' she said, 'let's go someplace else.'

'Sure,' I said. 'But I don't have a car.'

'That's all right. I do.'

'Have we searched her car yet?' said O'Meara to the uniformed officer.

'Yessir.'

'Then we're done for now,' said Mrs. Andrews. She turned to me and said, 'Let's go.'

'First, if you don't mind, I'd like to inspect the body.'

'You're not going in there, Rick,' said O'Meara. 'My men are working right now.'

'Right, so you're not going to let me see the body.'

'That's right, Rick.'

'Let's just leave,' said Mrs. Andrews.

'Listen to the lady, Rick – beat it.'

'All right, O'Meara. This is low, though.'

'Bye, Rick.'

I sat shotgun beside Elaine Andrews as she drove her black BMW fast. The dashboard looked like it belonged in the cockpit of an airplane. The seats were black leather. They were comfortable, the car was comfortable. For a moment I wondered why I don't drive. Is it because my mind wanders? Is it because I know that if I drove that's how I'd die, behind the wheel of a car? This car, though, made me rethink my driver's licence, or rather my lack thereof. The night was dark. It was a little after midnight. The bare tree branches, too, were darker than the night. They hung over the road and looked like they were going to sweep the windshield like the brushes at the carwash, I thought, while we drove fast along the dark road to a destination unknown. I hadn't asked where we were going. It didn't seem to matter, as she drove her BMW fast along the dark road with the black branches. Mrs. Andrews looked at me, then back at the road ahead. She was younger than forty, I thought, though it didn't matter. She might even be younger than thirty. What I knew for certain was that Gerald Andrews was older than her, significantly older – sixty, at least, I thought – and very wealthy, and I could tell that simply by their possessions, what little of them that I'd seen, and by the way they lived in general: the house, the cars, the furniture, the front porch. The voice on the phone, when she first called, though altered by tears, still didn't match the person sitting beside me, not hysterically crying but driving. The voice, the woman, they didn't match up, I thought, though I'd hardly heard her talk, except for over the phone. She broke the silence.

'Will it affect your solving the case, not having seen the body?'

'I don't know.'

'It was terrible,' she said.

'Where are we going?'

'For a drink. I need a drink.'

'Okay, but where?'

'A small bar, not far from here.'

The talking stopped.

The bar was small indeed, and long like a railway car, though it was wider. It was dark, too, except for a small yellow electric candle with a red plastic shade on the tabletop and dim white Christmas lights surrounding the bar. I ordered a double Scotch, neat, and Elaine said, '*La même chose, s'il vous plaît,*' for the waitress was French. Elaine was truly beautiful, I thought, looking at Elaine. She looked like a film actress, one from the sixties, a brunette, though I couldn't remember her name. We drank for a few minutes without saying anything, though Elaine didn't seem uncomfortable. Elaine seemed okay – happy, most likely, to be out of her home, where her husband's dead body still lay, I thought, or at least it was still there when we left her house. The Scotch was good and it was strong, not watered down in the slightest. No one gave any indication of recognizing Elaine Andrews but I suspected she frequented the bar. It seemed like she found this dark bar, with its few patrons, a relaxing atmosphere, which I found it to be, too. The music was soft and hard to make out but sounded good nonetheless. The drinks smelled strong and warm. Despite the fact that I was on the job, I was having a good time. It'd been a while, as long as I could remember, since I'd sat across from a beautiful woman, one who looked like a foreign film star from the sixties (she was foreign, the film star I was thinking of), drinking fine single malt Scotch neat. The drinks smelled good and the music was nice and Elaine looked radiant and it felt good to have company, for I hadn't been on a case in a while, and I'd just been drinking, reading and working on my old case notes at home for weeks, maybe even months – for as long as I could remember. We were both hesitant to speak. Eventually, she spoke first.

She started by asking me questions, questions about detective work (how long had I been a detective? what makes someone choose that sort of career?, et cetera), questions about my personal life (was I married? did I live alone?, et cetera), and I answered her questions in an attempt to put her at ease, with the hope that she'd start talking, too. I told her that I lived alone and that I'd never been married. I told her that I'd taken an interest in detective work from a young age – from a young age I'd thought about my future detective work, my cases, my chronicling, my solving, when there was something to be solved. I talked mostly, while she asked the questions, and we drank a few more drinks. Slowly, I started slipping in questions, too: 'When did you meet your husband?' I asked. 'Where did you meet him?' I asked. 'How long were you married?' I asked. 'What did he do for a living? That is to say, how did he come about his considerable wealth?' She answered the questions as they came – some curtly, some extensively – but she kept asking me questions, too. She said she'd met her now-dead husband, Gerald, six years prior to his death, in a resort town out west, where she'd been working as a ski instructor for about two years. She gave him a lesson, she said, and he invited her out for a drink, after the lesson, and she said sure, she said, and they had a drink at the chalet and she said she found him charming, witty and self-assured. I sat up straighter when she said *self-assured*, then felt embarrassed. She said that he wasn't aggressive, though she knew he wanted to sleep with her. She said, although she'd never dated a man his age, or even kissed a man his age, she felt curious about him, even though he was older. 'Younger guys get boring,' she said, and I simply nodded. 'They're selfish and often idiotic,' she said. 'They guard their time jealously, and then waste it on inanities.' Much of what she said hit a nerve, or at least made me tense up a little. She said that it was nice to have a drink with someone who had his life together – or seemed to – and she was referring to the time she'd first met Gerald, when she had had drinks with him at the ski chalet, after his ski lesson, not to having drinks with me, in the narrowish bar, after her husband's murder. If it was murder, which it of course most likely was.

They were married quickly, about four months after they met, in a small chapel in the mountains, outside the resort town where she'd worked. She'd quit her job as soon as they got serious, she said, which was about two weeks after the initial ski lesson. At that time, she said, six years ago, Gerald had just acquired a company that made plastic bottles from recycled materials, a company he sold, shortly after they were married, for a substantial profit. That's what Gerald did, she said: 'He bought companies that were in trouble, he invested in them, then sold them for profit.'

'In the six years you two were together, can you tell me some of the companies he owned?'

'Sure,' she said. 'But he wouldn't always own the companies outright. Often he'd invest with a group of investors, though sometimes, occasionally, if it was a small company, or a restaurant or something, he'd be the sole investor.'

'Would the investors he went in with always be the same group of people?'

'Often, but not always. There were a few, though, whom he worked with often.'

'I'll need a list of those names.'

'Sure,' she said.

She told me about the bottle plant, the flour mill, the sawmill, the restaurants, the ice cream cone factory, the tire factory and all the other different types of businesses that Gerald had invested in. He was very rich, she said, richer than he let on – and he didn't live frugally, I thought, from what I'd seen, even though he didn't live in a mansion. It was a nice house, though, a good size, not too big, and the location was excellent. They had two BMWs in the driveway, too, but Elaine said Gerald could've easily afforded a fleet of BMWs, and I imagined that, a fleet of BMWs …

She said, 'Can I tell you something, Rick?' And I said, 'Sure, but my name's not Rick.' I told her that the R. in the R. James Detective Agency ad stood for Robert, and Elaine said that she hadn't seen the ad, and that she'd called me Rick because Detective O'Meara did. 'O'Meara's an asshole,' I said. She agreed. I asked her what she'd wanted to tell me and she started telling me a story that Gerald, her now-dead husband, told her when they met.

They were in the lodge, sitting by a roaring fire, drinking expensive XO cognacs. It was snowing outside and getting darker but the snow kept things light. Gerald, after many drinks, while holding Elaine's hand, said to her, *Elaine, I'll tell you something my grandfather told me, shortly before he died of lung cancer. He said to me,* she said he'd said, *'Gerald, take what you can get! Don't end life in the negative. You want to outdo your grandfather – and your father – because you want to be in the green, not the red, when all's said and done,'* she said he'd said. Gerald told Elaine that his grandfather had told him that morality's a lie, through and through, and simply an impediment to man's success. Gerald said that he thought his grandfather was harsh but that much of what he'd said was true. *'Weak people, people who stand to lose something, try and convince you that it's wrong to do whatever it is that might hurt them,'* she said he'd said. *'That's how you know you're a threat, if people tell you that what you do can't be done – that's when you know that you're getting somewhere!'* she said he'd said.

'Gerald's grandfather, his father, Gerald – they were warriors,' Elaine said, 'for better or for worse.'

'For example?' I said.

'Gerald read people well, for example, and would have nothing to do with them if and when they tried to use him or cheat him. He wouldn't directly confront them, necessarily, but he'd have his revenge. Success. He made a lot of money. Same with his father. Same with his grandfather. *De père en fils.* But Gerald made more money than either of them.'

'Did you ever see Gerald behave aggressively toward anyone?'

'Many times,' she said.

'Tell me about one.'

Elaine said that an old business associate, whom she refused to name, had made a deal, buying a small company, telling the seller that Gerald was in on it – so, trading on Gerald's name, though he had no intention of telling Gerald. Anyway, she said, Gerald knew but played dumb, and then never let that guy in on a deal again, cut him off completely, and made sure others did, too, and basically ruined the man's life. Elaine dabbed at her eyes. The bar was almost empty but no one was pushing us to leave. We kept ordering drinks but Elaine said she didn't want to talk about Gerald anymore, or his business affairs, which weren't that interesting, she said, though he travelled a lot for work. I asked her about her childhood, where she grew up, though she answered only what she wanted to answer. Her maiden name was Jefferies. Elaine Jefferies. She grew up in a small rural town, surrounded by other small rural towns, which together made up quite a large county, a county she didn't get out of much, but while living in said county, she said she covered every square kilometre. She loved the open spaces. She said it was beautiful, especially when the clouds' large shadows drifted across the golden wheat fields. Her childhood was on a farm, though her father worked in town, too, as a pharmacist, and they kept livestock. Her teenage years were wild, she said, a lot of drinking, some drugs, a lot of sex. Her grades were always good, though, and she went on to university, for three years, and received a BA. She'd studied history and French. It was nice to get away from home, she said, but she didn't want to go on in school. And then she moved out west, and after two years, she met Gerald Andrews.

'And you know the rest,' she said.

'I don't know anything,' I said.

She was beautiful, without a doubt. I didn't want to ask questions about her husband or her former lovers. To some extent, I was jealous of her husband, even though he was dead. I told her we didn't need to talk about case-related stuff anymore. I told her that I realized she must be exhausted. She thanked me. We decided to have one more drink, then call it a night. She must've dropped me off at home. I woke up, on my couch, fully clothed.

2

One thing was clear to me shortly after waking, on my couch, fully clothed: namely, I was in love with Elaine Andrews née Jefferies. I brushed my teeth and gargled mouthwash in an attempt to rid my mouth of the acrid taste of several whiskies. I think I'm in love with Elaine, I thought. And she did drive me home, I thought. For a long time, though, I wondered if I'd tried to kiss her when she'd dropped me off at my apartment; or if I'd invited her up to my place; or if I'd tried to kiss her and she'd accepted, then came up to my place, and I'd passed out on her; or if I'd tried to kiss her and she'd told me to get lost; or if I'd done more than try to kiss her, if I'd in fact told her how I now believed I felt about her – that is to say, if I'd told her that I love her! There was no point in fretting, I thought, I'd know soon enough if I'd behaved badly; after all, she was my client – *she'd* hired *me* – so things would be okay, I thought. After brushing my teeth and gargling mouthwash I drank several glasses of ice water and then looked for Elaine Andrews's number in my wallet but found nothing save a receipt, no money and no number, and I remembered spending the last of my money at the bar, buying the last round of drinks, the last round of neat single malts. It surprised me that I didn't take down a number, a number where I could reach her, her cellphone number, for example. Her cellphone, too, had been sitting on the table, while we drank drink after drink and talked about her now-dead husband, Gerald, their brief courting period, his shady-sounding business dealings, and about her childhood and adolescence, a childhood and adolescence I found myself fantasizing about jealously, picturing the vast open spaces she'd described, the beautiful golden fields of wheat, the sun shining down brightly in the blue sky, with large billowing sun-spiked clouds moving fast over the vast wheat fields, while she had sex with boys in pickups and in said fields, as the clouds' shadows drifted across the golden seas of wheat. Elaine's youth seemed distant from me – distant and exciting and irreproducible. I imagined making love to her in the hayloft of her parents' barn. I imagined making love to her in her parents' farmhouse. I imagined making love to her now, in the back of her BMW, as I lay back down on my couch – I couldn't believe I hadn't gotten a number. She was my client, after all; perhaps, I thought, it would've been wise to have taken down a number where she could be reached. I did remember her address, however: 19 Tower Street. It was twenty minutes by taxicab, which wasn't bad. The cab came to $24.45, but I got a receipt, because I'm on a case. Even though I was in love with Elaine Andrews, I thought, I still had to charge for expenses, though I'd of course buy her the odd drink, and perhaps even dinner sometime. I hope she calls today, I thought, while lying on the couch, with my eyes closed, determined to sleep some more, determined to escape my hangover, and then I fell asleep for a few more hours.

When I woke up, I poured some juice, drank several glasses, and then I got into the shower. The washroom filled with steam while I washed and repeated fragments of conversation I'd had with Elaine silently in my head, though occasionally out loud. Elaine still hadn't called. I wondered again why. I must've embarrassed myself, I thought. I must've told her that I love her, I thought, told her that I love her on the day, not the day after or the day after that day, but on the day her husband was found on the couch with a knife in his chest. I exposed my loathsomeness, after several Scotches, to Elaine Andrews, I thought, in all its grotesquerie. 'What a stupid thing to do,' I said. The water was hot and the washroom filled with steam while I clutched my head under the near-scalding water. She'd told me about her love for her now-dead husband and I responded by saying, 'I love you,' though she spoke French, so I might've even said something as stupid as '*Je t'aime,*' I thought, as I stood under the hot water in the steam-filled washroom while clutching my head. '*Je t'aime,*' I said. '*Je t'aime, mon amour.*' Though I might not have said anything, I thought. I might've been on my best behaviour, and acted gentlemanly, even though I love her. Perhaps because I love her, I thought, I acted gentlemanly. I thought hard, hoping that I'd behaved gentlemanly, while I finished my shower in the near-scalding water.

'The phonebook,' I said. I knew her address – 19 Tower Street – so *the phonebook*! (If I didn't drink, I thought, perhaps I'd be a better detective.) Under a small pile of books sat my stack of phonebooks. I searched my most up-to-date phonebook and sure enough, under her name – not Gerald's – was their number. I wrote it down on a yellow Post-it and stuck the note beside the phone. I wondered what I would say. I wondered how to engage her. I wondered if I should begin by apologizing for drinking so much while on a case. I'll tell her I won't drink for the rest of the case, I thought. Until this case is finished, I will no longer drink, though that might be a difficult promise to keep, for it's impossible to know for certain how long a case will go on for; many remain unsolved, as I've said already, and then there's no end … I stared at the number and thought about dialing, and what I'd say, what I'd say to Elaine, when she answered. There's no need to feel embarrassed, I thought. Your job's to solve a case, not to worry about how you're perceived.

I decided to record the conversation for my records. I set up my recording device and tested it before calling Elaine. I called a local florist and asked how much it'd cost to send a bouquet of flowers to 19 Tower Street. The florist, who was a woman, a woman of approximately fifty, I guessed, though I was probably wrong, asked me what kind of bouquet I was looking to send and I said I was looking to spend around twenty dollars. She said, 'For delivery, you have to spend a minimum of forty dollars.' So I said, 'Okay, for forty, what could I get?' She asked me what was the occasion and I said I wasn't quite sure and then she asked me if it was for a wedding or a funeral or just because and I hesitated and then said just because. She told me that for forty dollars they'd put together a very lovely bouquet, a mélange, though mainly made up of purple lilies. I said that sounded perfect. She asked me whether I planned to pay with Visa or

MasterCard. I told her that I'd call her back re the flowers later and so on and so forth. Then I listened to the playback.

The recording, the recording of the conversation between me and the florist, was crisp and clear and the device worked perfectly, as I'd expected it to, though I wanted to be thorough, so as to make sure. I looked at Elaine's number and although I was nervous – my stomach felt weak and my heart beat quickly – I knew that I must call her and suss out the situation. I needed to know, I thought, where I stood, even if it meant discovering something unpleasant about myself. Before I called, though, I went and poured a large glass of ice water.

3

*(**T**ime: 1330h. Place: My apt. I pick the phone up off the mount, look at the number on the Post-it [i.e., Elaine Andrews's number], and I key said number into the number pad. The phone rings approx. four times before she picks up. I've already started the recording device.)*

EAnéeJ: Hello …

RJ: Hi. Elaine. It's me. Robert. Bob. Bob James. The detective.

EAnéeJ: Hi. I was wondering when you were going to call. How are you?

RJ: A little hungover, actually, though fine. And I've resolved to cut way back on my drinking for the remainder of the case.

EAnéeJ: Don't do anything crazy. [*She laughs.*]

RJ: Did I … ? Did I do anything crazy last night?

EAnéeJ: No. I did, though. I drove home.

RJ: I shouldn't've let you.

EAnéeJ: You tried to stop me. You tried to tell me not to drive, that we'd order a cab, that the bartender would order us a cab. I didn't listen. It was too late, so I dropped you off, and you said I could crash at your place, that you'd take the couch, but I said goodnight and drove off. Anyway, I made it home fine, thankfully, though it was dumb of me to drive that drunk, especially … Anyway, it's over now, and I promise to watch my drinking and driving.

RJ: Well, I'm glad to hear you made it home safely. What's going on at your house?

EAnéeJ: An officer stopped by this morning, though no one's around right now. Oh, wait … [*indeterminate background noises*] Sorry … Sorry about that … Do you want to get together?

RJ: Soon. What did the officer from this morning want?

EAnéeJ: He was going through Gerald's desk, and he was taking pictures for his report, he said. I asked him what he was looking for and he said any evidence that would help the police department catch the killer. He took photographs of Gerald's desktop, as it was, covered with files, letters, journals, magazines, random notes with messy handwriting, and he kept taking pictures. He asked me questions, though I avoided answering them, because I've already answered those questions: *Where were you when your husband was murdered? What cause would someone have to murder your husband? Did you and your husband ever fight?* they ask. They ask all sorts of demeaning questions, the same ones, over and over, ad nauseam. He was checking me out, too.

RJ: Who? The officer?

EAnéeJ: Yes. He was looking at my body, up and down, in a creepy way; he was leering, shamelessly leering, while I stood in my husband's den, waiting for him to finish and leave. He looked at me and said, 'So you stand to inherit a sizable amount of money. Come over here,' he said and stupidly I obeyed, and he motioned for me to lean in, and then he whispered into my ear, 'Now that you have all the money and don't have to fuck the old man you must be pleased.' I told him to get out. He laughed. I screamed, 'Get out now!' He tried to talk so I screamed more, 'Get out, get out, get out!' I screamed at the top of my lungs and then eventually he started backing out of the house. The neighbours to the right of us, the Walton-Fischers, were standing in their driveway, wondering what was going on. The officer got in his squad car and I didn't stop screaming till he was gone. It felt good to chase him out of my home.

RJ: You did the right thing. He sounds like a maniac.

EAnéeJ: You should come over here. I don't like being alone here right now.

RJ: Perhaps you should stay with family or friends while this investigation's underway, for the next few weeks at least.

EAnéeJ: I have no family anywhere near here, and I have no friends I want to stay with. I want to be in my home, even though Gerald was murdered here – I won't be scared away. Why don't you stay here, too?

RJ: I should keep some distance from things.

EAnéeJ: Think about it. Anyway, come over soon.

RJ: I will …

EAnéeJ: Bye.

RJ: Bye.

(*Call terminated at 1336h. I return the phone to its mount shortly after pressing the* END *key.*)

4

Flowers, I thought, weren't such a bad idea after all. I called the florist, whose shop was just down the street, and I asked if I were to go through with my order, for forty dollars, to 19 Tower Street, could I maybe get a lift with the delivery driver. She asked me where I live and I told her and then she said, 'Okay, sure. He'll pick you up in twenty minutes.' I prepaid over the phone with my Visa and asked for a receipt. While waiting I brushed my teeth again and reapplied underarm deodorant and sprayed on a little eau de toilette, a gift from a former girlfriend, and I also put on a clean shirt, even though the other wasn't dirty, because I wanted to appear fresh, despite the hangover. The delivery driver will be here any minute, I thought, and I put on my coat and grabbed a notepad and pen, put them in my inside pocket, and I grabbed my keys, with a small penknife and small flashlight on the keychain. I drank two glasses of ice water. I wondered whether I was forgetting anything, then I grabbed my wallet. I grabbed my sunglasses, too, remembering what a friend's uncle said to me once: 'Never leave home without your wallet, keys and sunglasses.' I looked at my watch and decided to wait out front for the flower delivery driver, since he was doing me a favour.

The delivery driver showed up in a small black hatchback, and the back of the car was full of bouquets. The passenger-side seat, too, had a large bouquet on it but the driver, Darren, made some space for it in the back. Darren was tall and slim and I'd guess seventeen, though he told me on the car ride that he studied philosophy and history at one of the local universities, so he was probably around twenty, if not a few years older than twenty; nevertheless, he looked like he was seventeen. He asked why I don't drive and I said it's because I don't have a car or a driver's licence. He asked what I did for a living and I told him that I'm a private detective. I thanked him for picking me up. 'No problem,' he said. The car, obviously, smelled of flowers; at first it was pleasant, though as Darren drove, slowly, I started to develop an acute headache.

I said to Darren, 'Do the flowers ever get to your head?'

'Yeah,' he said. 'All the time. Crack your window.'

I opened my window slightly, so as not to damage the flowers.

'You have a headache?' said Darren.

'Yeah,' I said, 'though I'm also hungover.'

Darren drove fast and told me a story about a philosopher, one from a small mountain village, a hundred-odd years ago, who leaves his cottage and goes into town so as to get some flour, sugar, eggs, milk and meat, if there is meat, from a store that a friend of his, a philosopher too, runs from home. The two philosophers meet – Philosopher A, the one who leaves his cottage to go get supplies, and Philosopher B, the one who runs a small shop out of his home – and talk for hours about politics, science, art and love and drink mugs of some sort of mead. Philosopher A's convinced, Darren told me as he drove, that love as such, that love *qua* love, is nothing more than misfiring Spirit, Spirit clouding one's senses, confusing one and leading one astray, that is to say, blinding one: blinding one as a prisoner. But Philosopher B says, Spirit's what clouds your so-called senses, for it's what grants you the ability to imagine love in the first place. Love, too, can confine, he says, yes, true. But so-called Spirit, the fantasy of Spirit, this is necessary to possess the illusion, to be able to even have illusions – to generate more illusions one need be inhabited *ab initio* with so-called Spirit, says Philosopher B to Philosopher A. I know, says Philosopher A, that's why I think love's a lie. If Spirit's present in the beginning, as a sort of initial state, then once illusions are acquired, begetting more and more illusions, in time some illusions – ones based on non-truths, of course – transmogrify, *mutatis mutandis*, into exalted love. If this exalted love's born from lies, lies generated by Spirit, then *eo ipso*, he says, love's a lie. Although love may be a lie, as you yourself say, says Philosopher B to Philosopher A, it does bring to light some certainties on occasion. For example? says Philosopher A. Well, for example, after loving – while loving, even, from time to time – we can be sure that we are really separate, that some sort of commingling, even temporarily, a commingling of Spirit, never becomes one. We are always separated, says Philosopher B to Philosopher A, who responds by saying, You're probably right. Then Philosopher A tells Philosopher B about a young man, a man in his late twenties, who is visited one night by the Devil. The Devil comes to the young man, he comes to him on a street corner, and says to the young man as he's walking: *There are things you'll never know, as I'm sure you already know, things beyond your comprehension, and there are things you do know, things you have no idea you know, and it's impossible for you to free yourself of this knowledge, although this knowledge is beyond your comprehension, too.* And then the Devil laughed, says Philosopher A to Philosopher B, said Darren while driving me and the bouquet to Elaine's. I asked Darren what the young man said in response. He said nothing, Darren said. I asked Darren what Philosopher B said to Philosopher A after the story, and Darren said he said that although it's important to recognize the bottomless pit in others, it's also important not to be dragged into that hole, and that although we're separate and alone, it is in fact possible to drag someone into a pit. Then Philosopher A said, *Omne verum vero consonat.* And that's it, said Darren. We pulled up to Elaine's house and I thanked Darren for the ride and the story and then I asked why he told me this story, and he said he wasn't sure, that he'd just read it somewhere, and that he wanted to see what I made of it, seeing as I'm a detective. I told him I wasn't sure what to make of it, though I'd think on it. I tipped him the few dollars I had in change. He said thanks and gave me his card and I took my bouquet and he drove off in the flower-filled hatchback.

Elaine answered the door dressed in jeans and a black woollen turtleneck sweater. She said hello and then sneezed. 'Gesundheit,' I said. She thanked me. I handed her the bouquet. I told her that I'd picked it up for her. She said she loved lilies. She seemed genuinely surprised and touched. This was my first time entering the Andrewses' home. It seemed bigger on the inside than it did from the outside – much bigger, in fact. I followed her into the kitchen where she was drinking a cup of steaming tea. She offered me one and I accepted. She asked me if I take sugar or milk or lemon and I said lemon would be good, for there was a lemon out on a cutting board. We drank tea in silence and that was fine by me. For a minute, I even started to read the newspaper sitting on the kitchen table. A developer wanted to build on an ancient Cree burial site. Elaine started to speak and told me about phone calls she'd been receiving; when she picked up, the person on the other end wouldn't say anything, simply waited, waited for her to get frustrated and hang up, but she said she wouldn't hang up, that she'd give the person on the other end *a piece of her mind*, telling them that they're sick fucks to fuck with a woman whose husband's just been murdered, bloodily murdered with a knife to the chest, and that if they weren't such goddamn cowards they'd speak up, say their piece, then leave her alone. I asked her how many of these phone calls she'd received and she said seven. Seven over the past eight hours. I asked her if she'd told the police and she said, 'Fuck the police.' We sat sipping from steaming mugs of tea and I thought about the phone calls and the murder and wondered if they were related: it sounds counterintuitive, but she was a beautiful woman, I thought, one who might perhaps attract these kinds of callers. I asked her if she'd ever received calls like that in past and she said yes but not so many in one day, in the past they were spread out, spread out over days, weeks, months, she said. I asked her if the calls started after she married Gerald. And she told me she'd been getting the calls since moving into the house I was standing in, the house Gerald was recently murdered in, and then I asked if I could see where she found the body.

The living room was smaller than I'd expected, which was strange, since the house's interior I'd imagined to be much smaller from the outside but in general was much larger save the living room. The room was impeccably decorated, however, with a small elegant vase on a small side table and a painting on the northeast wall, a painting almost solidly dark, though there looked like there might be a town and a jetty, perhaps, seen from the water, from the estuary, on a dark and foggy night, though I wasn't sure what it was supposed to be. The couch had been removed. Its impression remained in the carpet. There was a coffee table, with no couch. There was the side table, too. Nothing was on either table – save the vase on the side table – but that was because the police took everything, Elaine said, and I asked her what'd been on the table and she said an ashtray and some magazines and books and so on. 'I don't know specifically,' she said. There was a large window looking out onto their backyard, though it didn't appear to have been tampered with. Elaine said that it was shut, too, last night, the night of Gerald's murder. I stared out the window, onto the Andrewses' well-maintained backyard, thinking about the case and, more specifically, thinking about Elaine, who stood beside me, looking out the window, and I caught her looking at my reflection in the window when I looked up and at hers. She looked back out onto the yard. The sun was setting and the bushes and lawn looked dark and green in the setting sun. I yawned, unintentionally, and registered hunger. I hadn't eaten in a long time. Possibly days, I thought. The remaining leaves on the trees flapped in the wind but through the thick window we couldn't hear either the flapping of the leaves or the howling of the wind, if in fact the wind was howling, which it probably wasn't, for the leaves flapped gently, from the looks of it, from the living room, where not twenty-four hours ago Gerald Andrews had been stabbed to death. I looked over at Elaine's reflection again and again caught her looking at mine in the windowpane. I wondered what she was thinking. I hoped she was thinking, *I like him*. That seemed doubtful, however, despite the connection we were forming; no, she was probably wondering what I was thinking, whether I was currently solving the case, while staring out onto the lawn, lost in thoughts, thoughts re the case, while she stared at my reflection, wondering what I was thinking, thinking about the case, perhaps, or thinking about her; it was quite possible that she was wondering what I made of her, while I stared out the window, onto their nice backyard, sizing her up in my head, while she watched me do so. I think she thinks I suspect her, I thought. When she was looking at me, the first and second time, when she was looking at my reflection, the first and second time I caught her, both times, she averted her eyes quickly, perhaps nervously, though it was hard to tell, I thought. I'd hoped she was looking at me because she was attracted to me and couldn't take her eyes off me, though it was more than likely she was wondering what I made of the case. Re that, however, I didn't make much. I didn't know who killed Gerald and I had a few suspicions, but I was developing ideas slowly, piece by piece, all the while, of course, willing to dismiss my ideas, let them fade away completely if, for example, some more compelling ideas came along, though that wasn't happening, and everything on offer, for the most part, was unconvincing, as far as I could tell. No. There wasn't much to go on.

'Have you eaten?' I asked.

'No. My appetite's been pretty much nonexistent.'

'Well, nevertheless, we should eat,' I said.

'What would you like?'

'Is there any good takeout around here?'

'There's an excellent Chinese place near here that delivers. Mou Gui Fang. Szechuan and Cantonese but it's known for its Szechuan. It's spicy, a lot of it. Do you like spicy food?'

'Sounds perfect,' I said.

We couldn't decide between the Moo Goo Gai Pan or the Kung Pao Chicken so we went with the Moo Goo Gai Pan and the Kung Pao Ming Har, a similar dish to the Kung Pao Chicken, according to Elaine, but made with shrimp instead of chicken. We also ordered the Spicy Black Bean Beef, the steamed vegetables, two orders of steamed rice, two vegetable spring rolls, two Hot and Sour soups, an order of Szechuan Spicy Noodles and the Chef's Special Pork. Elaine said she had plenty of wine and beer or anything else we might want to drink. I offered to put the food on my credit card but Elaine insisted that she wasn't going to have me spend my money, not while I was a guest in her home, she said, not while working on her husband's case. I thanked her.

We sat in the kitchen drinking ice-cold beer while waiting for the food. Elaine looked tired. I was tired, too, but the beer was doing me a world of good, though at first it made my heart beat a little fast. Elaine twirled her hair while she flipped through the newspaper (*The Examiner*, i.e., a local rag). She looked up at me looking at her and took a sip of her frosted beer. She looked young, I thought, while she looked at the paper and played with her hair. She didn't seem to mind my watching her. Perhaps she liked it, I thought, perhaps it made her feel safe, having me watch, while she was reading, ensuring that she was safe to do so, safe from obscene callers and knife-wielding murderers. The truth be told, however, I don't carry a gun, nor do I own one, though I'm not bad in hand-to-hand combat. I took nine weeks of jiu-jitsu a couple of years back. I remember the moves. I do push-ups and sit-ups every day, too, like a man doing time.

The doorbell rang and we both perked up in anticipation. I offered to get the tip but when I opened my wallet there wasn't any money, since Darren, the flower delivery driver, hadn't stopped at an ATM. In all fairness, however, I never asked him to.

'Don't worry,' Elaine said, before it became an issue, 'I'm putting the tip on my card.'

I followed Elaine into the foyer and when she opened the door, it was, to my dismay, O'Meara.

'Good evening, Mrs. Andrews,' he said, accompanied by another officer, one I'd never seen before. 'Rick,' he said, 'you're still hanging around?'

'Till I solve the case.'

'Well, we have that to look forward to, Danny,' he said to his sidekick. 'Mrs. Andrews, we just need to ask you a few more questions about last night. It'll only take a minute, I promise.'

'All right,' she said, 'but I want Mr. James in the room.'

O'Meara sighed and said okay, then asked Elaine if she was in fact positive that she'd spoken with Mr. Andrews, that is to say, seen him in person, yesterday evening, after they'd had dinner together and he'd gone out. Elaine said that when he returned home he'd called out to her from downstairs, greeting her, and she'd called back, and that she hadn't actually seen him, though she did hear him come in and call out to her and she'd answered, then she fell asleep shortly thereafter, while waiting for him to come to bed.

'As I said last night,' she said, 'and this morning. I haven't changed my story, Detective O'Meara.'

'I thought you said you saw Mr. Andrews last night.'

'I did see him, when we ate dinner together at home, and then he had to go out for a few hours, and when he returned I was already in bed and he called out, "Hello!" and I called back. Then, while waiting for him to join me, I fell asleep in my bed for about an hour, and when I woke up, Gerald wasn't there. I felt around in the bed and I felt that I was alone. I called out his name. I called it a few times. When he didn't answer, I got out of bed and put on my robe and went downstairs. First I checked the kitchen, because the kitchen lights were on, but he wasn't there so I continued on. I checked his den and every light was off except his desk lamp, and it looked like he'd been there working moments ago. He wasn't there, however, so I went to the living room and there he was, lying on the couch with a knife protruding from his chest. Then I dialed 911. How many times do I have to tell this story?'

Despite Elaine's obvious exasperation, this was the first time I was hearing the story in full. The night before, when we were drinking, she didn't want to talk much about the case and I respected her decision because her husband had just been murdered and I was falling for her.

'We're just trying to be thorough, Mrs. Andrews,' said O'Meara. 'We want to make sure we have all the details straight.'

'I know, and I appreciate that, but my story hasn't changed since last night, or this morning, for that matter.'

'I'm sorry, Mrs. Andrews, I know you're under a lot of stress, but you and I haven't spoken yet today,' said O'Meara.

'Right, but I did talk to the officer this morning,' she said.

'What officer?'

'I don't think he ever gave his name. The one who was taking photos of Gerald's desk. The one who was riffling through the files. The one who harassed me.'

'Mrs. Andrews, I'm sorry, but I didn't send an officer here this morning,' said O'Meara.

'Then who was it? Who was in my house?'

'I'm not sure but we'll get to the bottom of this. Don't worry, Mrs. Andrews, we'll take care of everything,' he said.

I looked at O'Meara and told him he was doing a bang-up job so far.

'Shut your trap, Rick! What have you done? Where were you this morning?'

'O'Meara, you jackass, you should have someone watching the house. Her husband was murdered here last night. What were you thinking, that because they spared her last night no one will come back? You should have a squad car out front round the clock.'

'Don't tell me how to do my job, Rick. I've got everything under control. Mrs. Andrews, not only am I going to put a man out front, I'm going to have a man in the house at all times, starting tonight. I'll have someone sent over now.'

'Thank you, Detective O'Meara, but a man out front will suffice. Mr. James will be staying here this evening, so there's no need for an officer in the house.'

'Are you sure, Mrs. Andrews? Rick here's just a private dick. He's not exactly a trained professional. I bet you he doesn't even carry a gun – do you, Rick? Do you have a gun?'

'Yes,' I said, lying, 'but not on me.'

'I rest my case,' said O'Meara.

'Thank you for stopping by, officers. Good evening,' said Elaine.

'All right, I'm putting a man out front, though.'

'Thank you,' she said, and they left.

With her back up against the shut front door Elaine said, 'I was really hoping it was the food.'

We returned to the kitchen and finished off our beers, which were no longer ice cold.

I said to Elaine, 'I know you're sick of talking about this stuff but eventually you're going to have to fill me in on the details I don't know. I need all the details of the story, from A to Z.'

'I know. You know most of the story already. Gerald and I ate together, at home, and then he went out, and when he came home he called out to me and I called back and then I fell asleep and you know the rest …'

'What did you eat for dinner?'

'Sorry?'

'What did you and Gerald eat for dinner? Did you order in or did you cook or did – '

'We made dinner together. A simple pasta, a penne arrabiata, nothing fancy, a lot of garlic and a lot of chili peppers.'

'Did you drink?'

'Yes. We split a bottle of red wine, a Chianti. It was good. I drank more than Gerald, which wasn't uncommon.'

'So you ate dinner and then he went out immediately thereafter.'

'Not immediately, no. He went to his den and was on the phone for a while. I brought him an espresso. He likes espresso after dinner. I mean, he *liked* espresso after dinner. I don't. It keeps me up. I finished the wine.'

'Did he tell you where he was going?'

'No. But I didn't ask. He just said he'd be back in an hour and I said okay and then he was gone. I finished my wine and then got into bed and read for about half an hour and then I heard the front door open and shut and Gerald called out to me and I called back and I fell asleep and I woke up and then found his body and so on and then I got drunk with you and so on and then a police officer, who probably wasn't even a police officer, basically harassed me this morning, while I was suffering a terrible hangover, and then a crank caller kept calling me and then you came here and then that asshole O'Meara came and asked the same goddamn questions over and over again and I feel like I'm going crazy,' she said.

'I know. I'm sorry. I don't want to cause you any additional anxiety, you know. I want to help you but it means knowing everything you know about what Gerald was up to. Do you know who he was talking to on the phone?'

'No. I have no idea.'

'Did he seem upset when he left?'

'Not at all.'

'Did he go out in the evenings often?'

'Sometimes, though never for long. I didn't keep a leash on Gerald, and for that matter, he didn't keep one on me. Or at least I wouldn't let him.'

I wondered what that meant. Did it mean she had a lover? I wanted to ask and I think she knew that I wanted to ask. I was silent. I was thinking about the possibility of Elaine having a lover (or *lovers*, plural). For some reason, despite her beauty and the age difference between her and Mr. Andrews, I hadn't considered the possibility that she in fact had a lover (or lovers). I believe I paled. I should ask her, I thought, for it pertains to the case. If she has a lover, of course, he'd be a suspect, and so would she for that matter. I looked at her. Her wide-open brown eyes were looking straight at me. She knows what I'm thinking, I thought. She knows that I'm speculating about her sex life, I thought. It was pertinent to the case. I needed to know. I needed to know if she had a lover or several or none.

'Do you have a lover?'

'Is that really pertinent to the case?'

'Undoubtedly,' I said.

The doorbell rang. It was the delivery guy from Mou Gui Fang, with our food.

5

The food was incredible, like Elaine said it would be. The shrimp, the rolls, the soup, the Kung Pao Ming Har, the vegetables, especially the vegetables, which had been pan-fried, pan-fried in a sort of spicy soya sauce, I thought, but wasn't sure, being no chef myself, though I have a few dishes. I love water chestnuts, too, though eat them only when I eat good Chinese food. I ate ravenously but Elaine didn't eat much. We drank more beer while we ate and Elaine had wine, too. 'Eat more,' I said to Elaine, and she ate a little more, though mainly vegetables. The vegetables were incredible, and I wanted more, too, but she finished them off, which was of course fine. Since I'd asked her if she had a lover, we hadn't said much to each other. That was fine, though, because I wanted her to eat something, but, of course, I kept wondering, wondering about a lover, but the food was so good that it briefly calmed my cursed imagination. When I was finished eating, however, I immediately imagined her with some young guy, someone athletic and vacuous but fun to fuck, as far as she was concerned, someone to fool around with when the old man was away, or perhaps even around, I thought. I felt jealous and angry, then looked at her, at her beautiful face, while she ate vegetables, and I hated myself for feeling jealous and angry, especially because I didn't even know her till yesterday, I thought, yesterday evening, when I took a cab to her home after she called me re the case. She was beautiful and I was lonely and something inside of me ached, gently at first, but persistently, and I realized I was making an expression of frightened and sad concern. My forehead furrowed, my eyebrows on strange diagonals, I confronted my feelings for Elaine and realized they'd bring me more hurt and heartache, for they already were, that is to say, already bringing me hurt and heartache. I feel like a jealous lover, I thought, but I'm only her private detective.

'I had a relationship,' she said. 'But not anymore. We stopped seeing each other a while ago. He was the one Gerald cut off, so to speak, the one who traded on his name.'

'When did you stop seeing each other? Why?'

'After Gerald cut him off,' she said. 'He became desperate and Gerald knew about us, though he didn't say anything, that was his style, but instead worked at ruining Adam's life, little by little, he picked away at it. He never trusted Adam in the first place but my affair with him just confirmed his suspicions. It was a mistake.'

'What?' I said. 'Getting involved with one of his associates?'

'Yes, that, but Adam specifically; if I hadn't've gotten involved with him, Gerald wouldn't've destroyed him financially, and Adam wouldn't've killed himself.'

'When did it happen?'

'When I realized that Gerald was making things difficult for him, I stopped seeing him, hoping that'd calm Gerald down. It didn't, though. Gerald just sped up his plan to destroy Adam. He made sure no one would do business with him and he found ways of reclaiming what belonged to Adam. Adam kept trying to contact me but I wouldn't answer his calls or his emails or letters. It was too much for me. I didn't realize how desperate he actually was. I was sad and thought he was just suffering like me and that we couldn't help each other while we suffered and so on. I just thought that it'd be healthier for him not to hear from me, but that wasn't the case. About a month after we last spoke, he walked down to the harbour late at night and drank a bottle of whisky, then walked out onto the frozen river and jumped in where there was a large crack in the ice. He left me a letter, though I didn't get to read it. Gerald intercepted it and burned it in our fireplace. He burned it in front of me and told me it was an irrelevant letter from an irrelevant ex-colleague of his. I knew it was from Adam, of course, but didn't argue with him. I didn't question him. From that day forth, however, things between us were never the same.'

'But weren't they bad already? Wasn't that the reason you had an affair in the first place?'

'No, not at all.'

'Then why did you cheat on him?'

'Because there was something about Adam that was different from Gerald, it was different and exciting, and I loved him for that, for being different and exciting, for treating me differently, for not always keeping me at arm's length.'

'Did you want revenge for Adam's death?'

'Yes,' said Elaine, 'but I didn't want Gerald to die. I don't think he knew how desperate Adam really was. I don't think he thought Adam would kill himself. It wasn't his fault.' She paused, drained her wineglass, then said, 'If it's anybody's fault, it's mine.'

I didn't argue with her or say anything, hoping that she'd say more, though instead she stopped talking and poured another glass of wine. I helped her clear the table and put the leftovers in the fridge.

6

'Do you want vodka?' she said.

'Sure,' I said.

'Would you like a martini or straight from shot glasses?'

'Shots are fine.'

She poured two and said, '*Santé,*' and I said, '*Na zdorovye,*' and we clinked the small glasses and drank back the freezing-cold vodka. She looked at me and smiled. I smiled back.

'One more,' she said, and I agreed.

It was getting late and we were drinking vodka so that maybe we'd sleep. We talked a bit, though about nothing of note. We smiled at each other and then drank another shot. After three, I put the bottle back in the freezer and poured us both large glasses of ice water. My hands were cold from the cold vodka bottle and the ice cubes. I went to give Elaine her water but instead I put it down on the counter and took her face in my cold hands and kissed her. She kissed back, so I kept kissing.

After a minute, she stopped and said, 'Let's go up to bed.' I nodded and followed her up the staircase; for the first time I was upstairs, but I was distracted. The room was large, the sheets dark, and that was all I noted.

7

'Your chest is hairy,' she said, nuzzled up against me, her hand on my chest and her head on my shoulder. My eyes were closed as we lay in bed, still dazed – I was not yet ready to consider the implications of sleeping with my client, a client whose husband had been murdered approximately twenty-four hours prior to my sleeping with his widow. Elaine, too, seemed to possess a sort of post-coital obliviousness, for she seemed softer, warmer in general, and very trusting, I thought, more trusting than before.

'You don't like hairy chests?'

'No, I like them. It's comforting,' she said. 'When I was younger I never thought I'd like hair on men but now I do.'

'Yeah?'

'Yeah. In my early teens I liked effeminate men, or at least hairless ones, but eventually that changed.'

'So you liked the kinds of guys who'd be in boy bands?'

'Exactly,' she said.

'Newts.'

'Right.'

'And now you like the Magnum PI types.'

'Not exactly,' she said, laughing, and I said, 'Good. I don't like those types, either. I don't even drive.'

Elaine then asked me about girlfriends, that is to say, if I had a girlfriend. Not anymore, I told her, the same response I'd given the night before. She asked me when we broke up. I told her we broke up about eight months ago or so, though I wasn't sure. She asked me what happened and I told her that when we first met there was a series of misunderstandings, resulting from her blindness, that led her to believe I was a millionaire, and that at first things were blissful, like they'd never been before with anyone else, for either of us, ever in our lives, but then eventually, after our initial courtship, a surgeon claimed that he could cure blindness, or at least the type that she suffered, and he was performing free operations, so she contacted the surgeon and got the surgery, and then when she discovered that I'm not the man she'd imagined me to be, that I'm not the millionaire she'd imagined me to be, we both realized that things would never work out for us and that a life together would be impossible. 'It was sad,' I said, 'for both of us.'

'Uh-huh,' she said. 'So what really happened?'

'I'm not sure,' I said, and must've sounded sincere, for she let me leave it at that. 'There were girls before her, though.'

'Oh yeah?'

'Yeah.'

'How many?'

'Girls have I slept with or had serious relationships with?'

'Had serious relationships with.'

'Not that many, though they seem to get more serious each time,' I said, 'but I suppose that's how it goes.'

'For a while,' she said.

And we left the conversation at that. We were silent for a long time, though not sleeping, just lying in bed, in each other's arms, without talking, thinking, perhaps, though it was hard to be sure. For a while, I wasn't thinking, but then I began thinking about Gerald Andrews again and wondering if his killer was in my arms, though I didn't really believe Elaine was the killer, or at least I didn't want to believe that she could possibly do such a gruesome thing to someone she loved, or at least once loved, according to what she'd said. Could I ever kill someone that I once loved? I wondered. Of course, at times, I've thought that it'd be easier if someone I once loved were dead, rather than separated from me, but those kinds of thoughts are fleeting, at least in my experience, like all thoughts, though some turn into action. It's sick what some people do to leave their mark on an indifferent universe. No, I thought, I can't dismiss the possibility that Elaine killed Gerald – or had him killed – to avenge Adam's death. We become cold and hard when we're let down or angered, I thought, and we often lash out at those who we feel duped us. Elaine hadn't spoken in a while, though her eyes were open and unmoving, save the odd blink. We stared into each other's eyes as if into space. Then she opened her bedside drawer, produced a bottle of 222s, swallowed at least three, without any water, and again closed her eyes.

8

While Elaine slept I sat up awake trying to think what my next move would be. I really was at a loss: sleeping with her, not surprisingly, threw me for a loop. I knew I wanted to be around her, though, as much as I possibly could be, and that in fact was my plan, that is to say, to be around her as much as possible. I watched her sleep and felt a calm I hadn't felt for a long time, even though she might've killed her husband not twenty-four hours earlier. Her eyelashes were incredible. The idea of eyelashes once again became incredible to me, while I watched her sleep, breathing softly, her mouth slightly opened. Her lips looked dry and her face younger than when awake. I closed my eyes and thought of the image of Elaine sleeping; feeling unburdened, I drifted off.

9

When I woke up I was alone. I knew I was alone immediately, before opening my eyes. I felt around nonetheless. Elaine wasn't there. I sat up in bed. I looked around the room. I called out her name – 'Elaine, Elaine, Elaine.' I got out of bed and put on my pants and T-shirt and went downstairs, the whole time periodically calling out her name. She wasn't in the kitchen or the den or the living room. I opened the front door. Her BMW was still in the laneway, exactly as she'd left it. Across the street sat an unmarked police car, a blue Ford, and the officer behind the wheel perked up when he saw me at the front door. I waved and shut the door. 'Elaine!' I yelled. No answer. The house was silent save for a low-level hum. I was worried, though not yet panicked. I checked every washroom in the house. There were five. I checked every bedroom. There were four. I checked the unfinished basement, which was full of boxes of books and cobwebs and bottles of wine and old sports equipment, like baseball gloves and lacrosse sticks and cross-country skis and an old-style football helmet, for example, and there was a chalk portrait of a woman, a brunette, though it definitely wasn't Elaine Andrews. The woman in the portrait had light brown skin and brown eyes and wore a yellow dress from, I thought, the seventies. The background was light green. It was a nice portrait, actually, though obviously made by an amateur artist. There was an old microwave the size of a TV and there were boxes overflowing with old tableware. I went back to the main level. She wasn't in the house. I checked every closet. There were thirteen. Soon, if she didn't show up, I was going to have to notify the police. Nowhere in the house were there signs of forced entry, not in the living room or the den or the kitchen or anywhere else in the house. I checked the garage. There was nothing but firewood and motor oil and antifreeze and a snow blower and a lawn mower and two bicycles and rock salt and so on. I started panicking, my heart galloping, and as if a blinding white light exploded, charging through my mind and body, I thought: *I'll never see her again.*

10

'Listen, Rick,' O'Meara began, circling the kitchen table, where I sat silently, taking his bullshit because I felt on some level that I deserved it, 'I know your client wasn't the nicest woman in the world but you had a responsibility, Rick, a simple responsibility: to wit, to take care of your goddamn client if you're going to have a sleepover and especially if you're going to bang her. Did you bang her, Rick?'

I didn't acknowledge his question. I didn't acknowledge anything, for I was fading in and out of other thoughts. I thought about Elaine's and my life together, a life that would now never be, though I indulged some fantasies anyway, replete with our home and trips and perhaps children one day, and, later, grandchildren, and so on, but none of that would happen now. Nothing and no one would take the place of her, I thought. She's disappeared. I'd look for her, I thought, but I knew she was gone – vanished into the thin, suffocating air.

O'Meara continued chewing me out. 'I've got all my men looking for her,' he said. 'You'll lose your licence,' he said. 'I'll see to it.' He kept circling, without stopping, quickening his pace. 'I'll admit,' he said, 'Elaine Andrews is a bit of a See You Next Tuesday, but you were still responsible for her.' He continued circling the table, though I remained silent and immobile. I felt sick and weak. O'Meara, I could tell, enjoyed seeing me withdrawn and suffering and scared.

O'Meara was called away, thankfully, by a uniformed officer, the one from the night before. I, however, stayed seated. My stomach seized and nausea made itself known and the room started to spin in my mind and before my wet, bleary eyes. I clutched my stomach and took deep breaths through my nose. Eyes closed tightly, I tried to focus, focus on something, without success. My heart, too, once again raced. I tried to quell the urge to vomit and knew if I tried to race to the washroom or the kitchen sink or the garbage I'd never make it. Slowly, I took deep breaths. I didn't want to take in too much air at once and vomit as a result. I counted my breaths. I tried to slow down all thought. Nevertheless I thought about Elaine and her dead husband and feared she was dead now, too, as a result of my negligence stemming from overwhelming concupiscence. I thought about Elaine with a knife in her chest. It was too horrible – I concentrated on the infinite space created by my tightly sealed eyelids. *Elaine's okay*, I told myself, *Elaine's okay, wherever she may be, she's okay, she's okay*, I told myself, over and over and over again. I continued to count my breaths.

Eventually, my nausea passed, or at least abated, and I was still left sitting alone at the kitchen table, the table where Elaine and I had eaten Chinese takeout and flirted and talked about her dead lover and her dead husband. Bodies were piling up and I had no clue what was happening; Elaine's whereabouts were my only concern but my hands were tied till O'Meara let me go, I thought, but then I decided that if O'Meara was going to leave me unattended I was going to split. I stood up and started toward the front door. O'Meara was barking orders into his cellphone like a maniac and he screamed when he saw my hand on the front door's handle.

'Where in the goddamn do you think you're going!' he screamed, and I tried to ignore him, but a uniformed officer grabbed my wrist and O'Meara said, 'Cuff him,' and the officer quickly twisted my arms behind my back and clasped on the handcuffs.

'You have no right to do this,' I said.

'We'll take them off when you learn to stay put,' said O'Meara. 'Stick him in the office, where he won't get in the way.'

I sat at Gerald's desk, manacled, looking at the spines of the hundreds of books that lined the walls of his den: *The Warren Buffett Way, One Up on Wall Street, Buffettology, The Alchemy of Finance, Business @ the Speed of Thought, The Downing Street Years, Diplomacy, Years of Renewal*, and so on and so forth. *Who Moved My Cheese?*, by Spencer Johnson, M.D. He only reads books by successful people, I thought. *Where Have All the Leaders Gone?, Forbes® Greatest Business Stories Ever, The Reagan Diaries, My Life and Work: An Autobiography of Henry Ford, How to Win Friends and Influence People, Mein Kampf, The Wealth of Nations, The Prince, Leviathan, The Art of War* and so on. Plus he had two sets of encyclopedias: Britannica and World Book. He had some nice dictionaries in English, German, Italian, French and Spanish. It looked like he had a bunch of books on tape, too. I was stuck in Gerald's desk chair, handcuffs digging into my wrists, waiting for I'm not sure what. Gerald's dead, Adam's dead, and, most likely, I thought, Elaine's dead. At the very least she's gone. I wanted to get back to my apartment. I needed rest and time to think about the case. I'd gotten too close, obviously, and lost all perspective. I'd lost the forest for the trees, so to speak. Something had gone terribly wrong, beyond a shadow of a doubt. Something happened while I was trying to figure things out, while I was being, quite willingly, seduced by Elaine. So much escaped me. Everything changed while I had my head up my ass.

11

'Rick! Rick!' I woke up feeling far from refreshed. My nose stung as I inhaled. O'Meara was standing over me, holding the cherry of a lit cigarette directly under my nose. I coughed and gagged. My eyes stung, too. 'Rise and shine, sleepyhead,' O'Meara said. 'I'm going to uncuff you but you're not free to go. Understand?' He looked out of focus to my bleary eyes. 'Understand?' he said and pushed me.

'Yeah, yeah,' I said.

He released me from the handcuffs and I rubbed my wrists, like in the movies, I thought, and kept rubbing my wrists. They were red and chapped and sore and I felt generally sick. 'Can I get something to drink?' I said.

'I want you staying put in this office,' said O'Meara. 'Is that clear?'

'Clear as mud.'

O'Meara left and I sat rubbing my wrists. I was parched. My mouth tasted awful. I opened Gerald's desk drawer and inside was mainly just a mess of papers – bills and receipts mainly – and some business cards. I sorted through them quickly but only recognized a lawyers' card, Bouvert-Adamson (Bouvert was the name of the lawyer Elaine gave, I thought, when she first called), and I slipped it into my wallet. I looked around at the books and stood up and tilted my head and read the spines on the shelves. I pulled down a copy of *The Art of War* and opened it to a bookmarked page: '18. All war is based on deception,' it said at the top of the page.

O'Meara's voice and footsteps were approaching. I shelved the book and slid back behind the desk. O'Meara entered the office.

'Did you fuck her, Rick?' he said. I didn't answer. Again, he said, 'Did you fuck her?'

'No,' I said.

'Are you telling the truth?'

'Yes.'

'If her body turns up and we find *any* of your DNA, even a hair, a single pube, I'll make sure you're locked up for eternity.'

'Okay,' I said.

'This is serious, Rick. You don't sleep with your client when you're on a case. It's these kinds of stunts that kept you from becoming a detective.'

'I am a detective.'

'A real detective.'

'I am a real detective.'

'Right. Keep telling yourself that, Rick.'

After a few more minutes of O'Meara's bullshit he said I was free to go for the time being, stressing the point, *for the time being*, over and over again, and I said whatever you say, then searched my wallet for Darren's card.

I used Gerald's desk phone. Darren picked up after three rings. I asked if he wouldn't mind grabbing me – said I'd explain in person – and he said he'd be there in fifteen minutes. O'Meara watched me the whole time but I didn't give a shit. He didn't intimidate me. He never does, I thought, though he thinks he does. He thinks going to the academy and rising up through the ranks of the force to become a detective like him is what I wanted, but that's where he's wrong, I thought. I never wanted to be that kind of detective.

I sat on the front porch waiting for Darren. The police officers weren't so friendly and I was anxious to leave the scene of the crimes. Light pink clouds drifted westward in the sunset. Parts of the sky were a deep clear blue. Darren pulled up to the house in his flower-filled hatchback and lightly beeped the horn twice. He waved.

Right away I thanked him for picking me up and said, 'Let's get the hell out of here.' He nodded and drove off. I told him everything, for some reason, that is to say, I told him about Gerald's murder and Elaine calling, O'Meara, the narrowish bar, the surfeit of whiskies, waking up on my couch, receiving a call from Elaine, O'Meara again, dinner, drinking, sleeping with Elaine, waking up alone, the interrogations, the handcuffs and so on and so forth. Darren listened. I told him about what an asshole O'Meara is, about how we've never gotten along, even when we first met, though then we were civil.

'It sounds like you two are competitive,' said Darren, 'like your jobs are too similar for you to be friends – *odium figulinum*, trade jealousy.'

'Perhaps, though I've always felt that our methods and motivations – our *modi operandi*,' I said, showing him I knew a few words in Latin, too, 'are so different that it cancels out what our trades have in common. I don't even feel like we're playing the same game. Ours are different trades, in many ways.'

I still agreed with him, though. There was no denying that we didn't get along, without a doubt.

'Do you think Elaine's all right?' said Darren. I said that I wasn't sure. 'What's your next move?' Darren said.

I opened my wallet and read the address on the Bouvert-Adamson business card. 'I figure someone will still be at the office if we get there soon.' Although the sun was setting, it wasn't yet six o'clock. Darren said he could get me to their law offices in ten minutes. He said he knew the old building well because he'd photographed its gargoyles for an architecture forum.

'Actually, technically they're not gargoyles – they're chimeras,' he said. 'They don't spout water.'

I said, 'Cool,' and nothing else. We drove on in silence. Darren respected my privacy; he let me think, uninterrupted. I watched the city go by, anonymous buildings housing anonymous people, some of whom were up to no good. I didn't care, though. It was a Montreal that didn't concern me. I wondered, however, if Elaine was hiding out in any of those buildings or homes, holed up with a lover, one she never mentioned, not Gerald or Adam or me but someone secret, or at least kept secret from me – or perhaps she was being held in an apartment against her will, tied up, blindfolded, hungry, tired, scared, hurt, bloody or worse. We drove on to the lawyers'.

Adorned with menacing-looking gargoyles, or chimeras rather, as Darren had explained, sat the stout old building. It looked like a less dilapidated, though less benign, version of the old building I inhabit. Dark clouds gathered above it and its chimeras.

I was going to meet the lawyers, not knowing what to expect, not knowing what they knew, if anything, for Elaine only mentioned her lawyer, Bouvert, once, saying that he'd recommended me specifically, giving her my telephone number, though I'd never met the man in my life. I recognized the name but I'd never met the man. Darren pulled up to the curbside and said he'd wait.

'You don't have to. I can get a cab from here. I appreciate you grabbing me from the Andrewses' in the first place, but you don't have to wait.'

'It's no problem really,' he said. 'I'll wait. And if you don't come out in half an hour I'll come in and get you.'

'I think I'll be okay,' I said. 'It's just her lawyer.'

The elevator never came, so I climbed six flights of stairs to the Bouvert-Adamson offices. The reception area was large, with an empty waiting area to the side, with leather chairs and a table covered in current magazines. An attractive woman sat behind a sparse, tidy work station. Right away she asked if she could help me. I said yes and told her my name and that I'm a private detective, a private detective representing Mrs. Elaine Andrews in the case of her murdered husband, Mr. Gerald Andrews.

'Mr. Bouvert will want to see you right away,' she said, standing, and I said I figured he would.

Bouvert's office was large, too, with large windows behind his desk that looked out on the street. Everything was black leather. I sat in a large black leather chair in front of his desk. The walls were book-lined and there was a black leather couch and to its side a small locked metal cabinet in which I imagined he stored liquor and cash and possibly a gun. Bouvert was a large man, well dressed, wearing a dark grey suit, with a dark tie and what looked like black pearl cufflinks, though it was difficult to tell. He was bald and kept the few hairs he had close cropped.

He wore a heavy watch that I imagined was platinum with a pearl face. His teeth were bad. He didn't say much after introducing himself and shaking my hand. He motioned for me to sit down and then he sat down behind his desk. Leaning back in his chair, he stared at me in silence.

A younger, slighter man in a dark suit similar to Bouvert's entered the office. Bouvert looked at me and said, 'Bob, Al. Al, Bob.'

'Nice to meet you,' said Al.

I nodded.

'Bob here was the detective Elaine Andrews called after she found Gerald Andrews's body,' said Bouvert.

'Did you see the body?' Al said.

'No.'

'Are you sure, Bob?' said Bouvert.

'Sure I'm sure. I didn't see the body, even for a second. I hadn't been inside the house till yesterday, early evening, around five or so.'

Bouvert and Al exchanged knowing looks, though as to what they knew, I had no idea whatsoever. Al seated himself on the black leather couch. Bouvert stood up and walked around to the front of his desk and continued his questioning, resting his ass on the lip of his desk and leaning, saying, 'Did she mention anything about another man? Did she talk about any men other than Gerald?'

'I have a question first. Why'd you recommend me to her?'

'Pardon me?' said Bouvert.

'Why did you recommend me to Elaine?'

'I didn't.'

'She said that you told her to call a private detective, then gave her my number.'

'Mr. James, I'm sorry to contradict your story, but I never told her to call a private detective.'

'Then why did she call me?'

'I don't know,' said Bouvert.

Al sat silent and stolid on the black leather couch.

'Did she mention me to you at all?'

'Yes,' said Bouvert. 'Yesterday afternoon Elaine and I talked. She sounded withdrawn, but I expected as much. I asked if she wanted me to come over to keep her company, and she said that she'd called a private detective. She said you were on your way over. I asked her why she'd hired a private detective and she said that she wanted to get to the bottom of the case as soon as possible. I thought that made some sense.'

'What else did she say?'

'Nothing,' he said. 'I told her I'd call again soon and said goodbye and she said goodbye and that was that.'

Al remained mute and motionless.

'And that was the last time you talked to her?'

'Yes,' he said.

Bouvert seemed to be telling the truth. I didn't think he told her to call me, but some questions still remained unanswered: Why did she call me? Who put her in touch with me? Why did she lie, saying that her lawyer, Bouvert, gave her my number? I put these questions to Bouvert and his associate, but neither seemed to have the slightest clue as to why she had called or who put her in touch with me. When I began asking questions about Gerald, neither seemed to want to talk to me anymore. I insisted, though: 'Why would someone want to murder Gerald Andrews and target his wife?'

'Mr. James,' said Bouvert, 'Gerald's murder and Elaine's disappearance come as a great shock to us, too.' He walked around behind his desk and sat in his large chair in front of the large window. 'The truth is neither Al nor I have any idea whatsoever why someone would target the Andrewses.'

When I opened the door to the hatchback I asked Darren if he smoked and he said yes but we couldn't smoke in the car because of the flowers and because it belonged to the florist, so we sat on the curb and smoked cigarettes under a streetlight. I'd quit, years ago, though nevertheless I was smoking, not caring about the consequences, and my old cough reappeared immediately, a curt bark. I inhaled deeply, holding the smoke, then slowly exhaled the warm pinching smoke through my nostrils. My eyes were closed and I listened to the soft sounds of occasional traffic. Darren didn't talk. He was a nice kid. Respectful of others. I stood up and crushed the cigarette underfoot, thinking, I don't need anymore goddamn cigarettes in my life. A city bus approached and I said to Darren that I could take the bus home and he said that he was going my way anyway, and we got in the car.

We drove off and I turned to Darren and said, 'Thanks for waiting, bud.'

My apartment was dark and I didn't turn on any lights, just placed my keys and wallet on the mantel and went to the kitchenette and poured myself a drink and drank it back and poured another one, emptying the bottle, and dropped face down on my couch and kicked off my shoes and that was that.

12

A buzz startled me out of sleep and I woke on my couch, thirsty, listening to the rain on the fire escape. I remained still, then let my eyelids close under their immense weight. Again, however, there was a loud buzz. It was my doorbell. I sat up on the couch and grabbed the glass sitting on the floor beside it and held the glass up to the meagre light from the street; it was empty and opaque with fingerprints. Again, there was that loud grating buzz and I said, 'Hold your horses.' I stood up and did up my pants and belt and walked toward the door, unlocked it and opened it. Much to my chagrin, O'Meara stood there, with one of his plainclothes minions.

'Mind if we come in, Rick,' he said, as they pushed past me into my apartment.

'Make yourselves at home,' I said, lighting a cigarette.

O'Meara pushed me up against the wall, slapped the cigarette out of my mouth, and said, 'Don't get smart, smartass!' I shoved

O'Meara, and the plainclothesman punched me in the stomach. I dropped to my knees. I fought back vomit while trying to catch my breath.

'Now here's how it's going to be, tough guy,' said O'Meara, 'we're going to ask the questions and you're going to provide the answers. Understand?' I nodded. 'Did you rape Elaine Andrews?'

'Are you fucking crazy?' I said, and the plainclothesman kicked me in the left kidney, from behind, and I gasped in pain, clutching my side, gritting my teeth and waiting for the pain to dissipate.

'Did you rape her, Rick?' he repeated.

'You know I wouldn't hurt her.'

'Rick, we found your friend in a parking lot dumpster, the parking lot of a florist near you, Chez Marine, with her hands tied behind her back, gagged, and there are clear signs of forced penetration. Cause of death was a severe blow to the cranium. You wouldn't know anything about that – would you, Rick?'

'O'Meara, I didn't fucking kill her!'

The plainclothesman was holding up one of my boots, looking at its sole.

'Well?' O'Meara said to him, and he said, 'It's a definite match.'

'All right, cuff this motherfucker,' and the officer was on me, with his knee in my spine and my hands pulled around my back and clasped in handcuffs. The cuffs drew blood.

'You have nothing linking me to her death,' I said.

'Rick, you were the last person to be seen with her, one; two, we took plaster casts of the footprints in the Andrewses' backyard and guess what, buddy? That's right – your boots are a match!'

'I never set foot in the Andrewses' backyard.'

'You have the right to remain silent. Anything you say can be used against you in a court of law.'

'Fuck you.'

Someone punched me again in my kidney, and again I fell. 'Listen, you sick fuck, you're under arrest and you're going to rot in jail,' he said into my ear, both of us gritting our teeth, me in pain and him in anger, 'and I'll make sure you get bunked up with some twisted fuck who's going to ream you out every morning, every afternoon and every evening, you fucking scum!' My ear was wet with his spittle.

'You're a fucking moron, O'Meara,' I said, and then I was hit in the head with something hard and blacked out.

When I came to I was cuffed to a chair in a dark interrogation room under a bright hot light. I heard voices, though I couldn't see faces. 'Who do you think you're fooling?' said a voice. 'You're transparent as all hell. We know. We all know.'

'I have no idea what you're talking about,' I said.

'Playing dumb won't help you, Rick.'

'Hi, O'Meara.'

'Come clean, Rick.'

'Okay, I'll come clean. I think you're a fucking moron.'

A fist emerged from the darkness and caught the edge of my jaw. I bit my tongue when my teeth snapped shut and immediately tasted blood.

'We know what you're up to, psycho. There's nothing mysterious about it, you sick lonely fuck.'

I tried to talk but couldn't form words. Blood and saliva ran down my chin. The disembodied voices kept talking but I could no longer follow.

'I bibn't boo banybing,' I said.

'I bibn't boo banybing,' said O'Meara, laughing in the dark. And then he said, 'Work this degenerate over. We don't need fucks like this walking the streets,' and fists, many sets, emerged from the darkness and started pounding on my ribs, jaw and kidneys. My eyes shut tight, I gritted my teeth, and then I passed out from the pain.

I woke up, in the dark, still cuffed to the chair. The bright interrogation light was off. I called out and no one answered. I was alone. Immediately I thought of Elaine and felt sick. I pictured her, gagged, hands restrained, like mine, dead from head trauma. She was found in a dumpster, I thought. How'd she get there? How'd someone get her out of the house without me or the officer out front knowing, without making a sound or leaving a single trace? I looked hard into the darkness. I could make out nothing, which wasn't a surprise. I didn't kill her, I thought. I said out loud, 'I know I didn't kill her.' How could I? How could've I killed her, done away with the body, and made it back to inform the police? What was O'Meara thinking? A horrible buzz sounded and a red light flashed in the corner of the interrogation room. I stared up at it, frightened, and it kept sounding, over and over, and the light lit up again, and the room went red, then pitch-black, then red again, with the buzzing sound. I stared at the painted bulb. There was pounding at the door. 'Open up, Rick,' I heard, and the buzzing continued, now relentless, without pause, a solid grating sound, and the light stayed red, giving the room the horrifying atmosphere of a darkroom, where negatives, negatives of unspeakable acts, bloom into being. 'Open the fucking door, Rick!' And the pounding and buzzing continued. I tried to speak but couldn't. I tried to say, 'My fucking hands are cuffed!'

13

I woke up, fully clothed, on my couch. My doorbell buzzed loud and hurt my head. My mouth was dry and tasted bitter so I grabbed the glass beside the couch and took a big sip and then spat warm whisky on my floor. The buzzing didn't stop. 'I'm coming!' I yelled. Still, the buzzing continued. I stood up and went and opened the door. O'Meara and another detective stood there, still, and I said, '*Benvenuto.* I was just dreaming about you.'

'Don't play cute, asshole,' said O'Meara, and they pushed their way into my apartment.

'Why are you here?' I said.

'You tell me,' said O'Meara.

'I was sleeping. I have no idea.'

'Where is she?'

'Who?'

'Who the fuck do you think?'

'Elaine.'

'Good guess.'

'I have no idea.'

'Yes you do.'

'No, really, I have no idea. I woke up and she was gone. I called you.'

'In her bed.'

'What?'

'You woke up in her bed.'

'No.'

'You said you woke up and she was gone.'

'Yes.'

'So you're saying you were sleeping in a guest room and woke up and then went and checked in on her and she was gone.'

'Yes.'

'You're full of shit. You're a piece of shit.'

'Fuck you,' I said, and the other detective punched me in the stomach. I fell to my knees.

O'Meara said, 'Where is she?'

'I don't know.'

'Cuff him and let's take him in.'

Sitting in the back of an unmarked car, I tried to reason with O'Meara. I said, 'How could I have possibly killed her, disposed of the body and returned to call the police? The officer out front didn't see me leave.'

'He didn't see Elaine leave, either,' O'Meara added.

Still, though, I think he was taking my point. Why would I want to murder my client? Why would I want to hurt her, in any way, shape or form?

'I was duped, too. I'm as interested in solving the case as the police,' I said, and O'Meara made some disparaging remarks about my abilities as a detective. Then we stopped talking and his lackey drove us to the station in silence. We passed familiar buildings and I became lost in the rambling, nonsensical, relentless thoughts of someone who's nervous and exhausted. Nothing was coming together.

Then I said, 'She gave us the slip, O'Meara. She's disappeared. I don't know why but that's what's happened.'

O'Meara scoffed and said, 'Thanks, Rick, for your in-depth analysis of the case.'

I stared at the backs of their heads. My goddamn gaolers, I thought, two stupid assholes. They knew I had nothing to do with Elaine's disappearance, but O'Meara was keeping me captive out of spite; he resented me for innumerable reasons, all having to do with his deep sense of inadequacy, I thought. He was trying to teach me a lesson for sleeping with my client, I thought, a woman he would've killed to sleep with, given the chance, which he never would be – that is to say, be given the chance – despite being a *real police detective*. I had to say something, as we drove on pointlessly in silence.

'O'Meara, instead of wasting your time with me, you should be trying to figure out what's happened to Elaine. She's probably being held hostage right now – being abused – and you're wasting time fucking with me. It's ridiculous. Let's just find her!' I said and kicked the back of his seat.

'Pull over,' said O'Meara to his peon.

14

My downstairs neighbour knocked on my door to complain about my pacing, so I apologized. He thought I had people over. Nevertheless, moments after he left, I was back to pacing, though I removed my shoes. After pulling over to the roadside, O'Meara chewed me out and told me he'd let me go if I'd stayed away from the case. I agreed to his terms. Of course, it's ridiculous to think I'd stay away from the case – he knew that and I knew that – but I'd definitely try and keep my distance from him, I thought. I stood on the side of the highway trying to hail a cab but there were none. Eventually, I hitchhiked. Back at my apartment, I was upset and I paced. Somehow, I needed to see Elaine again. There was so much to discuss, but then again I wondered if she was even alive. She must be, I thought. There's no way a third party got past the officer outside and into the house, up the staircase, and stole Elaine away from the bed I was sleeping in, holding her in my arms, without making a single sound. It was an impossibility; therefore, Elaine left of her own volition. She knowingly escaped, I thought, for that was the only explanation that made sense. Why? I wondered. Well, first off, because her husband was murdered, so perhaps she feared for her own life, too, and wanted to make a getaway; however, perhaps she was involved in the murder and wanted to get away before I or the police discovered her involvement. The latter explanation, of course, made the most sense. Still, I didn't want to admit it. I didn't want to think that Elaine, this beautiful, funny and tender woman, could be involved in a murder, especially the murder of her own husband, who, presumably, I thought, she once loved. Murdering someone you once loved, however, I thought, makes more sense than murdering a total stranger. Nevertheless, I didn't want to believe she'd done it, or was involved in any way. By now, I thought, while pacing the long hallway of my apartment, she's probably fled the country, fled to São Paulo or Buenos Aires or who the hell knows where, with the money she's been stock-piling over the years, the years she was married to Gerald, after they met at the ski resort in the small town out west.

I needed rest but my mind wouldn't slow down. I thought about pouring a drink but decided it'd be better if I remained clearheaded. I lay down on the couch and stared at the ceiling, thinking, thinking about everything, and I was frightened – frightened that perhaps this woman was dead or a murderer: either scenario frightening, I thought. My eyes were heavy but I didn't close them. Staring at the ceiling, I wondered whether this boyfriend was really dead, if he'd indeed killed himself, or if he'd just disappeared, only to come back and help Elaine murder Gerald, and then flee with her after a night with me. I was back up pacing. I poured myself a glass of red wine from a lousy bottle I had in the fridge. I need to find out if Adam's dead or alive, I thought. I need to find out if Adam even exists. Adam's most likely an alias, I thought, and he's probably alive, too, and with Elaine Andrews this very minute. I must accept the hellacious possibility that she's with another man right this minute, I thought, while I paced my apartment floor worried about her safety, worried about a life without her. I've been played, I thought, like a big fat sucker. I downed the rest of my wine and then poured another glass. It was horrible wine, bitter and thick with sediment, but it was all they had at the corner store the night I'd bought it, the night before Elaine Andrews called me crying, crying over her dead husband, a dead husband I'm sure she conspired to murder. O'Meara's right, I thought, I'm an idiot – Elaine's stories don't jibe. For some reason, despite my cynicism, I fell for this woman instantly, without a moment's hesitation, and now I was paying for being an idiot, I thought.

Chain-smoking, I sat at my kitchen table in the dark. I'd finished the wine and was now drinking a can of beer, which was the only alcohol I had left in the house. This made me nervous. Everything was making me nervous. I took small sips of my cold can of beer, savouring it, knowing it would soon be gone and I'd still be wide awake, thinking about Elaine, trying to make some sense of what's happened. I listened to the playback of Elaine's and my phone conversation, over and over, studying Elaine's voice, rewinding the tape when it came to the end. The cigarettes were making me cough but I knew I wouldn't stop. I sat by the window and a cold wind kept blowing in as I attempted to blow smoke out. My beer was almost done. I knew there was no way I was going to get to sleep. I'd end up sitting in the dark, smoking, cogitating over the case, listening to the tape, getting nowhere. I decided to call Darren and see if he wanted to go for some drinks.

15

'Shots!' said Darren and I nodded. We drank whisky and beers. 'So what was the deal with this Gerald Andrews guy?' said Darren.

'I'm not sure, but it looks like he was up to some shady stuff, though I'm not sure how bad it gets. Definitely questionable business deals, et cetera. He was very rich but probably not the best of men.'

'*Honra y provecho no caben en un saco,*' said Darren.

'Sorry?'

'I'm sure he was an asshole.'

'Yeah. Seems like the type, not to curse the dead or anything,' I said. 'But he was probably bilking billions or something, I don't know. The guy was filthy rich. Do you want another beer?'

'Definitely,' said Darren.

I was getting drunk and was having a hard time following Darren. I remember he said something about some girl he had a crush on and something like, *now that blah and me're blah, we're blah blah.* That's all I made out. And in the background I faintly heard ABBA's 'sos,' though maybe it was just in my head. We stayed out late, though not surprisingly I don't remember much. We sat on barstools. There was some sort of shouting going on. Someone was arguing with someone else. But we ordered another round of beers. The more he drank, the more hyper and animated Darren became, as I became withdrawn, heavy and tired. I was seeing double. I picked up my beer to take a swig; the bottle left a ring of water on the bar, though the ring didn't join up. Darren was saying, 'Of the tens of thousands of days the average person lives, the majority of them are spent in a state of agitation and/or anxiety, or at least that's been my experience, in my give-or-take 9,000 or so days on Planet Earth, the only planet I know or will ever know most likely; perhaps my kids, if I have kids, or their kids, if my hypothetical children have children, will know a planet other than the one I inhabit but it's doubtful that I will and that's okay with me. You know?' he said and I nodded. I wondered whether Darren had been snorting cocaine. 'Before wars begin more male children are born and before they end more female children are born,' he said.

'Is that true?' I asked him.

'Yeah,' he said, and said he read it somewhere.

'What's happening now,' I said, 'are there more males or females being born?'

'In some societies more men are being born and in some societies more female children are being born – and in some species more males are being born and in some species more females are being born. So for some the end's nigh,' he said, 'and for some it's still a ways off. But I refuse to be a prophet of the apocalypse. There are enough of them around already, too many, without a doubt. So many people make money from selling the apocalypse. They're the custodians of the status quo.'

The shouting in the bar got loud, so loud everything else went silent. Some guy yelled at some other guy, *'You motherfucker!'* And then he attacked the guy with a pool cue. A brawl broke out and bottles started flying, one right past Darren and me that broke the backbar mirror. *'Sauve qui peut!'* a man called out.

'We better get the hell out of here,' I said to Darren and we skedaddled. As we slipped out, dodging fists and glass, it felt like we were escaping a fire, the bar roaring behind us. I thought I heard a gunshot but it was probably just a car backfiring, I thought. It looked like a few people were seriously hurt in the mêlée but we didn't stick around to find out. We staggered toward our apartments. Darren sucked on a wooden matchstick. I could've sworn I heard him say, *a something triangle-based pyramid looks like an electric vagina,* though I had no idea what that meant. He replaced the wooden matchstick he was sucking on with a cigarette and pressed his thumbnail into the sulphur head to ignite the match. He lit a cigarette for me, too, and after three drags I threw it in the wind, though it wasn't that windy, so it dropped pretty much straight to the ground. We walked by a drunken mendicant singing like a pirate –

Fifteen men on a dead man's chest
Yo ho ho and a bottle of rum!
Drink and the Devil had done the rest
Yo ho ho and a bottle of rum!

– as if he were marooned, without recourse to a ship or the sea, reduced to a pitiable landlubber.

'A seafaring man without the sea,' Darren said, and I told him I'd been thinking the same thing.

We talked and I slurred on about Elaine. About how I'd fallen for her. About how she gave me the slip. Darren listened politely as I made a fool of myself. I took a leak on a lamppost. I said to Darren in front of my building, 'I hate the fact that I spent so little time with that woman and I'm going to spend so much time thinking about her, stuck on her, probably for forever, or for my short forever … She really set me up and fucked me over.'

And Darren said, 'Don't let her, man – drop the case. Drop it like a hot potato.'

I dropped my keys several times before getting into my place. When I finally got in, I kicked off my shoes and fell face down on the couch – dead weight. Half asleep, I dreamed of Elaine. We sat at a small table at the railway-car-like bar, the one she took me to after her husband had been murdered, the one with the Xmas lights around the bar, where we drank single malts neat. She stared into my eyes. Pupils dilating, she leaned into me, palms pressed against the tabletop, she leaned across the table and whispered into my ear: 'The word *thesaurus* looks like it should be a type of dinosaur.' She sat back down in her seat. I watched her palm prints slowly disappear from the tabletop. I didn't see anybody smoking but saw a shadow of a stalk of cigarette smoke on the wall. 'Shake a leg,' she said. And then she told me that before her grandmother died, before her mismanaged diabetes finally killed her, she'd had her left leg amputated. She went into shock, she said, and became mute, so they gave her a shitload of Prozac or something to shock her out of her shock. For the year or so more she lived, she'd go to scratch her leg even though it wasn't there. 'She had phantom pains,' Elaine said. And I repeated, 'Phantom pains.' And that's all I remember.

16

I woke up before dawn and drank a glass of water while staring out the window. A torrential downpour – rain bouncing off the street. The window was open and the black curtains were filled with wind, swelling, and I looked at my reflection in the top section of the windowpane between the wind-parted curtains and thought of Elaine staring at my reflection in the windowpane at her house in the room where she'd found Gerald's dead body, lying on the couch, with a knife in his chest. She was with her lover somewhere, and they were both in on the murder. What else could've happened? It was the only explanation that made any sense, I thought, staring at my own weak reflection. I knew she fled because of her involvement in the murder but I couldn't help but think she'd disappeared under the impossible pressure of my desire. Somehow, even though I hadn't said anything, she knew I loved her – so she fled, I thought. Temporarily, time and space made sense because I was in love.

Or, rather, I thought I was in love, I thought. But she's gone now, I thought, and I'll never find her. The rain was loud like loud static and I tried to ignore the ghost of my image and concentrate on the water bouncing off the street, instead of my transparent reflection. I'm a huge sucker, I thought, an irremediable sucker.

I knew there was no way I was going to sleep so I worked on my notes. The insoluble is what keeps me going, I thought, it's what keeps detectives going, knowing our work is never done, never good enough. I decided I'd go see Bouvert and Adamson in the morning and find out if I could get anything on the supposed quote unquote Adam and see if anyone, anyone at all, involved with Gerald had killed themselves in the last year or so. Also, I'd stop by the flower shop and check in on Darren. He said he had to work in the a.m. I'd bring him a Gatorade or something, I thought. I worked on my notes and drank tea till the break of dawn, then I drank black coffee and showered and shaved and put on a jacket and tie.

17

Before walking to Chez Marine I drank another cup of black coffee and stopped at the corner store and bought Darren a blue Gatorade so he could hydrate. The boutique de fleurs takes only about ten minutes to get to on foot from my place. The streets were sunny and bright but I was wearing sunglasses. I was hungover but wired. I walked with the cold blue Gatorade in my hand and debated opening it and taking a sip but didn't. It was for Darren, I thought. I approached the boutique and saw myself in the glass storefront, holding the cold blue drink, and sunlight reflected back. I walked in and a small bell rang, quietly, and a woman with dark straight long hair looked up from cutting flowers and smiled.

'*Bonjour*,' she said, and I said '*Bonjour*' back.

Darren was in the back and spotted me and said, '*Julie, c'est mon ami Bob! Bob James!*'

'Nice to meet you, Bob,' she said, extending a small hand.

I shook it and nodded. '*Enchanté.*'

Darren came up to the counter from the back and said: 'Good to see you, man! How're you feeling?'

'Good, good. I brought you something,' I said, and threw him the blue Gatorade.

He caught it and said, 'Thanks, man! I really need to rehydrate,' and turning to Julie, '*On était un peu chaud, mais pas trop!*'

She smiled and nodded. Darren had started gulping down the Gatorade and Julie said, 'Do you need any flowers today, Bob?'

'I think I'm good today, for the moment at least.'

'They give him headaches,' said Darren, taking a break from his drink.

'I'm sure they don't all give him headaches.'

'What are those ones called?' I said, pointing to the ones she'd been cutting, the ones she'd been cutting when I walked into the store and she'd looked up from her task at the sound of the small bell.

'*Lis.* Don't you know *lis?*'

'Lilies, yes,' I said. 'Clearly not always by sight but I know them. I bought some from you the other day, over the phone – I ordered some. That's how I met Darren.'

'You asked for a ride with Darren. I recognize your voice from the phone.'

'I recognize yours, too. Anyway, sorry, I'm not good with the names of flowers. I couldn't tell a mallow from a hollyhock.'

She smiled and said, 'You have a very distinct voice. Have people told you that?'

'Yes, it's stupid sounding, right?'

'*Non, juste distincte, une voix distincte.*'

'You're making him self-conscious,' said Darren.

'No she's not,' I said, but she was. I stopped talking completely and just looked around at the flowers. It was a nice shop. I wished

I could list off the different types of flowers but the only ones I could name by sight were the typical ones, roses and tulips and I thought lilies (*lis*) but I guess not. The smell was wonderful but did slightly hurt my head, but then again I was hungover and over-caffeinated and sleep-deprived.

'Bob's a private detective. He's on a murder case.'

'*Mon Dieu!*' said Julie.

'It's true. A man was stabbed to death.'

'That's horrible!'

'It is,' I said. 'And it's possible that the wife did it, or might be involved somehow, but she's disappeared.'

'So now you're looking for her?'

'Yes.'

'Any leads? Clues?'

'Clues, yes. Leads, no. Not really, no.'

'Why would she want to kill her husband?'

'He was rich. She was much younger. The murderer could be a business associate. The murderer could be her – *sa femme* – but I'm not sure at the moment.'

'It was her,' said Darren. 'It's the wife.'

'*Pourquoi?*' said Julie.

'*J'ai mes raisons.*'

'*Quelles raisons?*'

'She fucked over Bob! She gave him the slip! She totally used him!'

'Darren!' I said, embarrassed.

'Well she did!'

'We don't know that.'

'We're pretty sure.'

'I'm not sure about anything,' I said.

'In this case, maybe you should be.' His forehead tightened and I became aware of the skull beneath the skin.

We said *au revoir* to Julie and went to make Darren's deliveries, before going to see Bouvert and Adamson. Darren looked rough and didn't say much. 'You holding in there?' I asked, as he coughed and weaved through traffic, looking dazed and possibly stoned. He looked skinny, I thought, even though I always thought of him as skinny, from the first time I met him, a couple of strange days ago. He was sweaty, too, as he zigzagged between cars. He didn't answer so I said, 'Are you okay, Darren?'

'Yeah,' he said, removing his hands from the wheel, rubbing his eyes, pressing his palms into his sockets, then heavily returning his hands to the wheel. 'I'm just hungover and tired. I'll be fine.'

'Do you want me to drive?'

'I thought you didn't know how to drive.'

'I know how, sort of, I just don't.'

'It's okay,' he said. 'I'm fine to drive.'

We pulled up to an office building, where Darren was delivering a bouquet to a secretary, he told me. 'The guy who ordered it sends bouquets to women all over town. Obviously women he's fucking,' said Darren. 'They're always attractive.'

He flicked on the hazards and got out and grabbed the bouquet from the back seat. 'I'll be fast,' he said.

'I'll wait here.'

I watched him enter the building and explain himself to a security guard and stand by the elevator bank, waiting for an elevator. I turned around and stared at the bouquets in the back seat. The colours were wonderful: the pinks and yellows, the greens and purples; red, dark stigmas and velvety stamens; bright filaments; and petals, thick and rubbery and thin and delicate. The diurnal morning glory and crocus, I thought, though I couldn't identify either species, and there probably weren't any in the back seat. On the floor sat Darren's red and blue knapsack. There was a small black notebook sticking out. I looked toward the lobby to see if he was coming out and then picked up the notebook and opened it up. Inside were random notes, jottings, doodles and poems. I read one and quickly copied it out in my own small notebook, though it slightly confused me. I read and then wrote:

> A brindled bull named Trucker.
> Mien.
> Anticlimactic, really, when you think about it.
> He used to be my friend,
> though not anymore:
> things got too competitive.
> It's too similar.
> Dreams of God,
> ineluctable and ineliminable.

I kept reading, periodically looking up toward the office building, toward the lobby, the elevator bank. The kid might have promise as a poet, I thought; I really had no idea but thought some of his notes and thoughts were funny, at least. There were some haikus, too, but I had time to copy out only one before Darren got off the elevator. I read and wrote:

> Love vanishes fast
> For some it never comes back
> That's where I am at

I quickly returned the notebook to the knapsack, making sure it was slightly sticking out, as Darren exited the building, approaching the hatchback. I wondered if Darren had recently had his heart broken. I wondered why he wrote that haiku – why he wrote haikus in general. Maybe he was just messing around in his notebook, I thought. Perhaps it had no great significance and it was simply silly, like lots of haikus. I wasn't sure. Darren got into the car and fell into his seat, heavily, I thought, for such a skinny guy, and he seemed exhausted and beleaguered. Darren possessed a sadness that I hadn't initially detected. Obviously, I thought, I hadn't been paying enough attention.

'If statements – ideas in general – couldn't be simultaneously both true and false, then communication – ideas in general – would be severely hampered.' Darren made this argument and I saw no reason to disagree. In fact, I was happy he was talking, for he hadn't uttered a word for at least fifteen minutes, while we were driving toward his next stop for delivery, a hospital. The bouquet was for a patient, not surprisingly, a patient who'd gotten in a head-on collision. 'Supposedly he's pretty banged up but going to be okay,' said Darren. He had no idea how the other driver was doing, he said. 'Ideas of an afterlife,' Darren was saying, 'are true as ideas, of course we have these ideas, but they're not true – we don't live on in these ideas.'

'You live on in other people's minds,' I offered lamely, and Darren said, 'Sure, yes, for other people, not for you. Mere imitations. You're dead. Your conscious mind is dead, your heart no longer beats and your lungs collapse.'

Perhaps, I thought, consciousness is ideology; perhaps it's that simple and that inescapable. I tried to express that to Darren but couldn't find the words.

'It's not that surprising that humankind's obsessed with apocalypse,' said Darren. 'You head toward death from the day you're born. Of course thoughts lead to destruction.' I had a coughing fit. 'Here we are,' Darren said, pulling up to the hospital, parking curbside: 'Death's Waiting Room.'

I told him not to be so morbid. 'The guy who got in the head-on collision's going to be okay, eventually,' I said, and Darren said that we still had no idea what happened to the other guy, then he flicked on the hazards and got out and grabbed the bouquet from the back seat.

'It's true,' he said, 'however,' leaning his head into the car, 'death isn't a one-time eventuality, of course.'

All day long the detective carries on this work, I thought, observing, weighing, comparing values of which he nor his client may know the significance. Somehow, this work does lead to solutions, outcomes, I thought, sometimes. Like looking through binoculars backward, what I was focusing on seemed vague and faraway, I thought, confused and distorted by false distance. Her thoughts were so far from mine, I thought. 'Where is Elaine?' I said and bounced my fist off the dashboard. I wanted a cigarette. I thought – erroneously, as it turns out – that there was something between her and me. Now I needed to track her down, I thought, as I stared at the hospital, where Darren was delivering flowers to a man who'd gotten in a head-on collision, survived, and was now convalescing, banged up but going to live. I kept thinking about smoking, nonstop. Some shamus I've turned out to be. Losing my only client and the woman I love in one fell swoop, I thought, staring at the hospital where Darren was giving flowers to a man most likely in traction. The thing about smoking that makes it so tempting, I thought, is that for generations cigarettes have been requested by countless numbers of people before they've been executed. Overhead I heard the thudding propellers of a helicopter, though I couldn't see it. I got out of the car and looked up at the greying sky, with purple cloud-banks in the distance, and saw the orange chopper heading toward the hospital's rooftop helipad. My head tilted skyward, I watched the chopper make its descent and disappear somewhere on the rooftop where I could no longer see it but could still hear the all-consuming propeller. The grey sky pulsed and throbbed under its hard beating of the air.

Darren returned in a much more chipper mood. He told me that the man, the man he was delivering flowers to, the one who'd gotten into the head-on collision, was in a full-body cast, with his left leg and right arm elevated. Regardless, he seemed like a great guy, Darren said, and he was high and happy to be alive.

'He said that. He said, "I'm high and happy to be alive." And he laughed. Cool guy,' said Darren. 'It turns out that the other driver's 100 percent fine, too,' Darren told me the man in the cast said. The man in the cast went on and on listing the things in life he's grateful for, said Darren, including waxing on about the breeze from the open window and about how said breeze made him think of when he was a kid, when he was around eleven or twelve years old, and he was sitting by an open window wearing shorts and talking to his then-babysitter, Marlene, and he felt the wind lightly blow up his shorts along his inner thigh and he realized that he had a hard-on, he said, and Marlene was laughing at something he'd said and she looked beautiful in the late-afternoon light and the breeze gently caressed his dick. He told Darren he's never felt so in love in his life and he's now married – not to Marlene – with three kids. He was really fucked up, said Darren, and they'd given him a shitload of morphine. And then Darren went on about how lucky we are to live in a world with drugs. I listened but was starting to doze off, dreaming of the mummified man in the hospital, who lay in traction dreaming of his former babysitter, past breezes and past erections. But then my dreams shifted. I thought of Elaine and hated the fact that I'd been used and duped by her. I felt cuckolded but she was never my wife and I've never been married. We needed to make one more delivery, then we'd go see the lawyers.

We drove past the cemetery first and Darren said, 'That's probably where they're burying the guy,' and in the distance I could see two gravediggers smoking cigarettes beside a backhoe. Then we approached the funeral home about five kilometres up the road. The parking lot was full and there was a hearse (black, of course, I thought) out front. According to Darren, the flowers he was delivering to the funeral home were from the firm the deceased worked for as a chartered accountant for thirty-odd years. We pulled into the U-shaped driveway and Darren parked behind the hearse. 'I'll be quick,' he said. 'They're used to me making deliveries and they're a really sombre crew, especially if there's a funeral in progress.'

I sat and stared at the back of the hearse and saw there was no coffin in it yet, and I kept wondering how many dead bodies it had transported over its years of service. The hearse looked to be at least a decade old, though it was in excellent condition. Clearly well taken care of, I thought – interior and exterior detailed often. It could be on the showroom floor, though it's approximately a decade old. So $10 \times 365 = 3{,}650$, I thought, and so let's say this funeral home (i.e., Everett Family Funeral Home Ltd.) performs, say, an average of two funerals a day (approx.), that's 730 funerals a year and 730×10 is 7,300 and so is $2 \times 3{,}650$. Is it possible, I thought, that this shiny showroom-quality hearse sitting in front of me has transported (approx.) 7,300 corpses to the graveyard or the crematorium (the funeral home having its own crematorium, according to the sign on the lawn) in its tenure for Everett Family Funeral Home Ltd.? The weather was overcast and the sunshine was long gone. I sat studying the back of the hearse and then wondered if Gerald's body was still lying in the morgue or if it'd been buried in the ground or burned up into ash. Most likely it's still lying in the morgue, I thought. A gruesome post-mortem performed so as to determine what we all already know, I thought, namely, he died from knife wounds to the chest.

Although I didn't see a single soul it was obvious that the funeral home was full. Darren exited the home and hopped in the car and said, 'Let's get out of here. The lawyers', ho!'

'First,' I said, 'I want to stop by the morgue.'

18

The morgue was in the basement of the hospital that the man in the cast was at so we had to double back, but Darren didn't seem to mind and it wasn't far. 'I haven't been here in years,' I told Darren as we took the elevator to the hospital's basement. I wasn't quite sure how I was going to get to see the body or read the autopsy report, but I felt confident that I'd figure something out. I'd bribe somebody, I thought, or pose as a police officer. For years I'd been carrying around a forged police ID in my wallet, always hidden behind my real IDs, et cetera.

I got lucky, however, for once: a doctor, Dr. Leonard P. Tate, was in the morgue, amongst the sterilized tools and galvanized-steel refrigeration units for cadavers. I told him the truth, or most of the truth. I told him that I'm a private detective, hired by Mrs. Elaine Andrews, the deceased's wife of six years, to speed up the process of solving this case so justice could be meted out swiftly, so the widow could start the process of moving on with her devastated life. Dr. Tate asked me what I wanted.

'First off,' I said, 'I was wondering if I could see the body?'

'That's impossible,' said Tate. 'The body was cremated late last night.'

'Doesn't that seem fast?' Darren said.

'Yes, but the autopsy was completed. I did it myself. There was nothing left to learn from the body. It was clear that he died from multiple stab wounds to the chest, more specifically,' Tate said, picking up the autopsy report from a table, *'perforation of the right lung and hemothorax causing intrathoracic and intra-abdominal hemorrhaging.'*

'Can I see that for a sec?' I said.

'No.'

'Please let him, doc,' said Darren. 'He's just trying to solve the case, same as the police.'

'I only want to glance at it.'

Tate looked hesitantly at the report in his hands and said, 'No. I told you everything you need to know. He died from stab wounds to the chest and sustained cuts on his hands from his efforts to defend himself.'

'It wasn't self-inflicted.'

'It most certainly wasn't self-inflicted.'

Darren walked over to Tate, popped the report out of his hands, and threw it over to me. I read,

AUTOPSY REPORT 91-06160

DEPT. OF CORONER: 0830h 13 October

DECEDENT: Andrews, Gerald

From the anatomic findings and pertinent history, I ascribe the death to: MULTIPLE SHARP FORCE INJURIES

ANATOMICAL SUMMARY

1. Multiple stab wounds of chest and abdomen: Penetrating stab wounds of chest and abdomen with right hemothorax and hemoperitoneum.

('Give that back! Security!' said Tate, but Darren held him back.)

2. Multiple abrasions, upper extremities and hands: i.e., Defence wounds.

EXTERNAL EXAMINATION

The body is that of a Caucasian male stated to be 66 years old. The body weighs 88.4 kilograms, measuring 182.8 centimetres from crown to sole. The hair on the scalp is grey and straight and sparse. The irises appear a sharp blue with the pupils fixed and dilated.

Both upper and lower teeth are capped.

There are no deformities but the decedent has a surgical scar on the left arm, from a reported surgery on a fractured elbow.

The body appears to the Examiner as stated above. Identification is by toe tag and the autopsy is not material to identification. The body is not embalmed.

The front of the chest and abdomen show injuries to be described below. The genitalia are that of an adult male, with the penis uncircumcised, and no evidence of injury.

(Tate was struggling and yelling but Darren continued to hold him back and I read fast.)

CLOTHING

The clothes were examined before and after removal from the body. The decedent was wearing a long-sleeved black sweater and white undershirt, both extensively bloodstained.

On the front, lower right side of the black sweater and white undershirt, there are long slit-like tears measuring 3.8 centimetres. Also on the lower right sleeve of the black sweater there is a 3-centimetre slit-like tear.

Decedent was wearing a pair of grey woollen slacks, bloodstained. The decedent also was wearing 2 black leather Oxfords and 2 black cashmere socks.

His underpants, too, are bloodstained.

EVIDENCE OF INJURY
DESCRIPTION OF MULTIPLE STAB WOUNDS:
1. Stab wound on right side of chest.

The stab wound is located on the right side of the chest, 45.7 centimetres below the top of the head and 15.2 centimetres from the back of the body.

(I skimmed and skipped ahead, while Darren restrained Tate.)

SHARP FORCE INJURIES OF HANDS

('Give it back,' said Tate. 'Now!' And I flipped ahead …)

CARDIOVASCULAR SYSTEM
The heart weighs 306 grams, and has a normal size and configuration.

(Tate broke free from Darren's grasp. I skimmed over the parts about the Gastrointestinal System, Hemolymphatic System, Urinary System, Male Genital System, Histology, Radiology – there was nothing pertinent to the case. 'I'm not kidding,' said Tate. 'Give it back now!' I quickly read the rest.)

WITNESSES
Detective Michael O'Meara, Robbery Homicide Division, was present during the autopsy.

(Tate ripped the report out of my hands and the last thing I read
was his name …)

   s/ LEONARD P. TATE, M.D., DEPUTY MEDICAL EXAMINER

19

As we drove toward the Bouvert-Adamson offices, Darren asked, 'Did you learn anything from the report?'

'No,' I said. 'Not really. Just the grim facts of the corpse, or what was the corpse.'

'Do you find it suspicious that they already burned the body?'

'Honestly, I'm finding everything suspicious. But there's little doubt that stabbing was the cause of death.'

'If he's dead.'

'Of course he's dead.'

'Have you seen the body?'

'No, but he's dead.'

'How do you know?'

'Darren, we were just talking to the doctor who did the autopsy. You were there. You knocked the autopsy report out of his hands and threw it to me and I read it. He died from multiple stab wounds to the chest – *multiple sharp force injuries.*'

'So you read the autopsy report … '

'Yes, I did. Autopsy report 91-06160.'

'But anyone could've written the report, Bob. It could be totally made up, or someone else's … '

'Doubtful.'

'They could've faked his death by giving him, like, hydrochlorothiazide or something to slow down his heart rate and then made it look like he was stabbed a bunch of times with makeup and – '

'It's far-fetched.'

'You haven't seen the body, is the point.'

'I see your point. But this would be a serious conspiracy that no one could pull off. You think the police are involved? O'Meara? You think good ol' doc Tate's involved, too? C'mon. Too many people. And why would Gerald Andrews want to fake his own death in the first place?'

'I'm saying it's not out of the realm of possibility.'

'We're pretty certain it's out of the realm of the possible.'

'No we're not.'

'Okay, we're not, I suppose, but it's unlikely. Highly unlikely.'

'Well, it's possible and I'm suspicious.'

'Good, I suppose. But I don't want to go down any wrong paths, you know.'

'Yes.'

'Anyway, you're right, though. I never saw the body. There were quite a few police when I got to their house, and that night the body was still presumably in the living room. It hadn't been taken away yet.'

'If there was even a body in the first place.'

'I think that we should presuppose that there's a body, or was a body, before they cremated it late last night.'

'But you didn't go in the house that night.'

'No, I didn't. I met Elaine on the front porch. She was giving her version of the events to a uniformed officer with a notepad, who was periodically jotting things down in said notepad.'

'So you stood on the porch and talked to Elaine and the officer.'

'Yes, and then O'Meara came out and we talked to him for a minute but then took off. We took off to a bar for some drinks.'

'Did you ask to see the body?'

'Of course I asked to see the body.'

'But O'Meara wouldn't let you.'

'No, he wouldn't.'

'*See …*'

'O'Meara wouldn't let me see the body because he's an asshole, not because he's tied up in some super-rich guy's conspiracy, Darren.'

'Still, the point remains.'

'It does but I think Gerald's dead. It's more likely she conspired to murder her husband or murdered him herself than that Gerald wanted to elaborately fake his own death, wouldn't you say?'

'I don't know. Maybe.'

'Well, it's more likely – much more.'

'Probably.'

'I'm operating under that assumption.'

'Well, that's all I was saying.'

'What?'

'That you shouldn't …'

'What?

'Operate under that assumption.'

'Okay, I won't. But the theory that Elaine conspired to murder her husband – or murdered him herself – is still the best theory I've got. We've got.'

'I suppose. But I'm not putting anything past these people.'

20

Darren and I sat in leather chairs in the waiting area of the Bouvert-Adamson offices: I flipped through magazines featuring wealthy people while Darren attempted to catch the attention of the attractive receptionist, Michelle, whose name he learned after introducing himself as soon as he saw her. She greeted Darren politely, even seemed amused, but that was that. I'd asked Darren to wait in the car but he wouldn't stay put. He said he wanted to meet *these lawyers* and ask them some questions himself. I told him I didn't think that that was a wise idea but he wouldn't listen and said this case was his problem, too, now. I told him it really wasn't and he said he wanted to help, that he'd been helping for days, and wanted more information. I said he could come up but told him I wanted to talk to the lawyers alone. He said that he couldn't make any promises. We sat and waited, and it seemed like Bouvert and Adamson were taking much longer than was reasonable, I thought, considering the circumstances. Darren, however, I thought, seemed unperturbed. Perhaps Darren and Michelle would fall in love, I thought, and that would be the only good to come out of this disaster. If that was the case, it definitely wouldn't be worth the trouble. Nevertheless, she didn't seem interested in Darren, though he kept periodically and unsubtly looking up and over at her. But Michelle diligently kept her head down, typing away, and her face glowed a soft blue in her monitor's light. When she finally looked up, I could feel Darren's blood charge with expectancy, though she just said that they were ready to see me. I stood and Darren stood, too, but I told him to stay put. He didn't protest.

Michelle walked me to Bouvert's office, and Adamson was there with him waiting for me. They looked guarded, I thought, when I entered the office, and I wondered if the gun I'd imagined to be in the small metal cabinet near Bouvert's desk was now somewhere on his person, or at least close at hand. I glanced over at the cabinet and it seemed slightly ajar, though it was hard to tell from my perspective. Nevertheless, I'd operate under the assumption that Bouvert was packing, I thought.

'Mr. James,' said Bouvert, the first of us to say anything, but he didn't follow up with any more words.

'You can still call me Bob.'

'What can we help you with?' said Bouvert.

'Do you know anything about Elaine's lover? Or *lovers*? This Adam guy who worked with Gerald. The one who supposedly killed himself. Do you know anything about him? I mean, now I assume Adam's an alias – obviously, of course. But do you know anything about her extramarital affairs, et cetera?'

Bouvert rested his interlaced fingers across his stomach as he leaned back in his chair and cleared his throat of the rich phlegm of a cigar smoker. His black cufflinks reflected back some light. 'Mr. James –'

'Really, Bob's fine.'

'Bob. Al and I think she had a lover, yes, of course. And he might've worked for or with Mr. Andrews at some point, too, but we're not sure. We certainly haven't heard of anybody who worked with Gerald having committed suicide. Or at least not anyone who may've been involved with Mrs. Andrews.'

The lover-who-committed-suicide-because-he-couldn't-live-without-Elaine story was most certainly bullshit, I thought, and I was irritated with myself for ever believing it, even for a second. 'Okay, I'll just ask the question straight up. Do you think that Elaine conspired to murder her husband? And, if so, do you believe she has a lover in on it?'

'What do you think, Bob?' said Bouvert, the one who did all the talking, while Al sat there looking skinny and menacing but distant.

'I think that she murdered her husband and took off with some dough and some lover to some far-off place.'

Bouvert seemed pleased and flashed his bad teeth and said, 'Al and I are of the same mind, Bob.'

When I returned to the waiting area, Darren was leaning on Michelle's station and they seemed to be getting along swell. Well good, I thought, because the lawyers proved useless. Darren and Michelle exchanged cards and we split. 'Did you learn anything from the lawyers?' Darren asked as we approached the hatchback.

'Not really, though they seem to think Elaine took off with some guy, too. But they have no idea who. Or if they do, they aren't sharing,' I said.

'Do you think they know more than they were letting on?'

'Yes, of course. Still, though, I'm not sure they know the identity of the other man. They said they didn't and I sort of believe them.'

'What else did they say?'

'Not much. One of them, Adamson, the skeletal one, he doesn't really speak at all.'

'Huh.'

'So you seemed to be hitting it off with Michelle.'

'Yeah. She might meet us for a drink later. I asked her some questions but she was reluctant to answer in the office, so I thought maybe we'd talk to her in a more hospitable environment over drinks.'

'Good thinking, Darren.'

'She did, however, tell me that Bouvert and Adamson are going for drinks in about an hour at the bar at l'Hôtel Athènes – le Charon.'

'Do you know who they're meeting?'

'A client. I don't know who. Michelle just said *a client.* She wouldn't tell me who. Said she wasn't allowed, though she let it slip that they had this rendezvous.'

'Okay, well, we'll have to trail them.'

'They know what you look like.'

'Yes.'

'But they haven't seen me.'

'Right.'

'So I propose I sit near them. I'm a good eavesdropper.'

'I wish I had my recording device.'

'I've got a notebook in my knapsack. I'll just take notes, you know, discreetly,' said Darren.

'Don't sit too close.'

'I won't. They won't spot me. I'll just have a drink and pretend I'm reading and taking notes. It's a hotel. They'll just think I'm a guest – someone's kid – if they think of me at all. I have great hearing. I can be discreet.'

21

Hôtel Athènes – le Charon. Tailing Bouvert and Adamson. Sitting near them. One's fat, one's thin. I'm assuming the fat one's Bouvert and conversely the thin one's Adamson. They've just sat down. The third man hasn't shown up yet. A waiter approaches them and takes their orders.

– *Bonsoir, messieurs.*

– Good evening.

– Would you care for some drinks?

– Yes, I'll have a vodka martini – on the rocks, in a rocks glass.

– Olives or a twist?

– Olives.

– Very good. And for you, sir?

– A CC and ginger.

– *Merci beaucoup.* I'll be right back with your drinks.

They sit silently eating nuts, esp. the fat one, Bouvert, the one who ordered the martini. They don't say a single word the whole time the waiter's off getting their drinks – and the waiter takes a while. The waiter returns and sets the drinks down on coasters in front of them, and more nuts …

– *Voilà, messieurs.*

Bouvert lifts his martini and says …

– Cheers …
– Cheers.

And they clink glasses. Then, Adamson, the skinny one, says …

– If he takes any longer I say we leave. We don't need him at all. He was incidental and ultimately inconsequential. Might be better to sever ties now.
– We'll hear him out. No need making enemies for no good reason.
– Even if he were our *enemy* – it wouldn't matter.
– Don't get so distressed. Really, we'll have a drink and hear him out and we won't deal with him for a long time to come.
– I can't believe he's late. The nerve of this fucking guy.

A few more minutes pass and they barely utter a word. They both, however, frequently glance at their respective wristwatches. Adamson seems pissed. Bouvert seems calm, drinking and snacking, unflappable. (I'm, by the way, drinking a beer, but it's in a glass and probably a rip-off. I hope to be reimbursed for incidentals!!)

They stir. A man in a dark blue suit with a raincoat folded over his arm approaches their table.

– Sorry I'm late.

– Why was that … ?

– Detective.

– What?

– Why were you late?

– Al, we don't need to worry about that.

– No it's okay.

– So …

– A case, of course.

– And …

– Some junky OD'ed.

– Why does that concern you?

– The boyfriend lived. They want to pin it on him.

– And the Andrews case?

– Yes.

– Any developments?

– Since she's gone AWOL?

– Yes.

– No, not really. It's quiet. I believe she's successfully made her getaway.

– Right.

– So what did you want to see us about?

– Well, business.

– Okay.

– I figure I'm owed a little more than I've received.

– Oh.

– Yeah, and –

– Let me stop you right there –

– Al, please let the detective continue. Go ahead …

– Well, I believe I've been helpful and feel I should be properly remunerated. Simple.

– It's not simple.

– I think Al means that we've already shown our appreciation; our mutual friend has shown appreciation for all your help.

– I don't want to know anything, still.

– And you won't. You don't.

– Without knowing, why do you think you deserve more?

– I know enough.

– I suppose you do.

– Yes.

– You realize you could be implicated?

– Yes. But no one will –

– No, you'd just be disposed –

– Al, please!

– Listen, I'm a police detective with Robbery-Homicide – you can't make those sorts of threats to me. Do you understand?

– You're not above anything, O'Meara.

– Do you understand? Do not threaten me. I can make your lives hell.

– He's sorry, detective. We've been under a lot of pressure.

– Tell me about it.

The waiter approaches the table and Bouvert and Adamson order another round and O'Meara orders a double Jameson on the rocks.

– Ballpark?

– We're not negotiating.

– I am, Al. Ballpark – what are we talking?

– A hundred.

– No way!

– Al.

– It's not that much.

– No?

– Considering …

– Considering what?

– How's about twenty. We could do that ASAP.

– It's a lot less.

– Yes, but as we said, we've shown our appreciation. This is extra, a bonus.

– Right, but I'm asking for a hundred.

– If it were up to me you'd get nothing.

– You'll get something, detective.

– Well, it's low.

– But you've already gotten an awful lot.

– Okay. Eighty.

– Eighty! You ungrateful motherfucker –

– Al, please.

– Eighty.

– Sixty, today, but then you don't ask for anything more – ever – and we forget we ever knew each other.

– That seems harsh.

– Those are the terms. It's the right thing to do.

– I can live with that.

The waiter returns with their fresh drinks and they say nothing while he places them on the table and collects the finished drinks.

– Okay. Let's have a drink to your newfound wealth, detective.

– Where do I pick up my package?

– Same place. Old Port. By the pier. Ten o'clock.

– Near that restaurant?

– Yes, I'll meet you myself with a briefcase, from the restaurant.

– *Eccellente! Salute!*

Bouvert and O'Meara clink glasses; Adamson doesn't.

– By the way, your friend, the PI, Mr. Robert James – Bob – he stopped by our offices an hour or so ago …

– Aw gawd.

– Yes.

– It's a problem.

– Nah. Don't worry, I'll take care of him. He meddles but he knows nothing, less than nothing, so he's not a threat.

– It's a problem.

– He's harmless – doesn't even carry a handgun!

– Detective, we –

– He's stuck in his own head. Really …

– It's a problem.

– I know he doesn't have a clue but I'll get rid of him. Don't worry.

– That's included in the bonus, right?

They all laugh evil-sounding laughs. O'Meara slams back his drink.

– Gotta run, fellas. But I'll be seeing you later.

– Don't be late.

– Ten o'clock.

– Good evening, detective.

– Okay, gentlemen – *merci et à bientôt!*

They watch O'Meara leave. Adamson says …

– He could've offered to pay for the drinks, considering how much he's milking us for.

– It's not your money.

– Nonetheless, he shouldn't get paid.

– Well it's only sixty more.

– Today. He should be eighty-sixed.

– So what do you propose we do?

– Well …

Adamson leans in and whispers something into Bouvert's ear for what seems to be an unnaturally long period of time and eventually Bouvert chuckles. He leans back …

– It's worth considering.

The waiter approaches and Bouvert hands him a black Amex. They leave shortly thereafter. I pay in cash. My beer, with tip, came to thirteen dollars!!

FIN

22

I sat reading and rereading Darren's transcript in the passenger seat of the hatchback in a state of disbelief. How could O'Meara be working for Bouvert and Adamson? I wondered, or rather: How could O'Meara be working for a client of Bouvert and Adamson? – a client who was more than likely Elaine Andrews, I thought, sitting in the car, a few blocks away from Hôtel Athènes, where Darren had followed the two lawyers into the bar, sat close and surreptitiously taken the minutes of their meeting with Detective Michael O'Meara of all people, a fucking fraud! In all the years I've known O'Meara I never had him pegged for being on the take, I thought, not to this extent at least. Sure, all cops are sort of dirty, I thought, enjoying the *perks* of the job – but this was different. This was aiding and abetting a murderer – or worse. I felt stupid for not having seen this coming, never suspecting O'Meara of *play this foul*. How much does he know? I wondered. Does he know Elaine's whereabouts?

'What the hell did he do?' I said and Darren said he wasn't sure.

'Well you did a good job, Darren.'

'Thanks. But we gotta figure out where this restaurant is, so we're there for the handoff.' Darren bounced in his seat, jacked up on adrenalin. 'Get the drop on the drop.'

'Well, Old Port, not far from the pier.'

'There're a bunch of restaurants around there.'

'We'll ask Michelle if Bouvert has a favourite.'

'Good idea,' said Darren and pulled out his cell and her card and called her.

While Darren sat, cell in hand, waiting for Michelle to pick up, I sat stunned. I felt amazingly stupid. I'd been deceived by essentially everyone, I thought, for the nth time, save Darren. But then I cast a sidelong glance at him, wondering if somehow, in some way, Darren was tied up in this conspiracy, in this web of lies, this hell I now inhabit, a hell I was dragged into with a late-night phone call while I was minding my own damn business and reading and drinking on my couch in relative peace. Could Darren be working for these goddamn lawyers and these rich assholes, these assholes who chew through people, masticating them, in service of their tawdry dramas and the further accumulation of vast wealth? Anything was possible, I thought, though I hated myself for having to always be so paranoid, though still never paranoid enough. I wondered what to do about O'Meara. Should I confront him before the handoff, or after the handoff, or at the handoff, at the pier, with Bouvert and perhaps Adamson, too? Also, I wondered, what was O'Meara going to do about me?

It seemed like an eternity as we sat there waiting for Michelle to pick up her cell. Darren had his cell up to his ear but I could hear it ringing, over and over again, while I sat there mildly suspecting Darren of being in on this strange conspiracy, one I didn't understand. The ringing was loud and I found it odd that a machine hadn't picked up yet, and the phone rang and rang *ad infinitum*. I didn't really suspect Darren, I thought, while listening to the abyssal ringing of the phone. But then I didn't really suspect O'Meara, either, and he was involved somehow, involved enough to be paid off to keep his yap shut. Clearly O'Meara was only partially involved, I thought, from what I could deduce from Darren's notes, since it was clear that he didn't know *everything*, and was ultimately *incidental* to the overall conspiracy, et cetera. That is, if Darren's notes were an accurate transcript of the conversation overheard at Le Charon. Perhaps, I thought, Darren's notes were entirely fabricated and scripted by O'Meara, Bouvert, Adamson and (I hated to think it) Darren so as to set me on the wrong path. I kept giving Darren sidelong glances as he held the loudly ringing phone to his ear. It was clear that Darren didn't suspect me of suspecting him, I thought, as he sat waiting for Michelle to pick up. No, Darren wasn't involved, he wasn't working for Bouvert and Adamson, I decided, and I desperately wanted to believe right then and there that Darren wasn't working for Bouvert and Adamson (or their client, rather, or *clients*, plural) and that he was in fact on my side, assisting me with the case, acting as my sidekick, a partner I could trust. Then, the loud ringing stopped and for a second there was complete silence.

'Hello … '

'Hey, Michelle, I'm sitting here with Bob and need to ask you a question … '

'Um, another time would work better.'

'I just need to know what restaurant Bouvert likes in the Old Port.'

'Okay, so later sounds good. Thank you.'

'Michelle, just think – does he have some place there he goes to often?'

'All right. Sounds good. Talk to you soon.' And she hung up.

Darren looked perplexed but I said, 'Somebody's with her. She can't talk.'

'Right,' said Darren. 'So what do we do?'

'We wait and call her back.' I rocked in my seat. I blurted out, 'When you call her back, though, don't ask questions – just give her a location to meet us at.'

'Right. Where?'

'A bar?'

'Okay, but what bar?'

'Shit, I wish I knew the name of the railway-car-like bar … '

'Where is it?'

'About twenty minutes east of the Andrewses' but I don't really remember.'

'Along the highway?'

'Elaine took a back-roads route. She drove for about twenty minutes and there it was alongside the road with the bare trees with the black branches.'

'Well, you're going to have to be more specific than that.'

'I know.'

'I know a place. A place we drink at after classes sometimes and I go there after work, too. It's a quiet dive. I'll tell her to meet us there in half an hour.'

Darren and I sat at a table in the bar by a large sliding window looking out on the street, waiting for Michelle. The plan worked, in theory; Darren called and told Michelle to meet us in thirty minutes at his bar, Chez Carlos, and all she had to say was *yes* or *no* and she said *yes*. Nevertheless, we'd been waiting for about thirty extra minutes and she still hadn't shown. For the first fifteen, I refrained from drinking beer with Darren and had a club soda with lime, but after fifteen I cracked and ordered a beer when Darren asked for his second. We sat there silently drinking our bottles of beer and staring off into nowhere, like the three or four other patrons. The bar was exactly as Darren had described it, a quiet dive. Punk rock music played softly and there was a pool table but no one playing and only men sat at the bar but the bartender was a woman, a thin pretty redhead, who looked tough, though, not to be fucked with, and the server was the only other woman in the barroom, a stout Québécoise waitress in her mid-forties, I'd guess, but I'm bad at guessing. Darren peeled the label off his second beer and used it as a coaster. He yawned, then rubbed at his eyes. I felt tired, too, but when was I ever going to sleep well again? This case, these people, they were devouring me, I thought, and I'd never rest well again. I stared out on to the street and it had started to rain.

I spotted Michelle walking in the rain with a black umbrella before Darren because she was walking north and I was facing south. She saw me and waved a small wave. Darren jerked around fast when he saw me wave back. She smiled.

Closing her umbrella and shaking off the raindrops, Michelle entered the bar and came over to our table. 'Hey, guys.'

'Have a seat,' said Darren and she sat down beside him, across the table from me. 'How're you?'

'Good, fine. Sorry about before, on the phone, but I was with Bouvert. He came back to the office after the hotel.'

'Do you know why?' I said.

'No, but it wasn't unusual.'

'Well the question remains,' said Darren. 'Do you know of a restaurant Bouvert frequents in the Old Port?'

'Yeah, of course. Diavolo Cucina, or its full name's something like La Diavolo del Cucina, but Diavolo Cucina, yeah … Italian … Bouvert goes there all the time – sometimes with Adamson but it's where he goes. I think he might even be a part owner or something, but I'm not sure.'

'That's helpful, Michelle. Thanks.'

She nodded.

'Have you ever been there with him?' asked Darren.

'Yes, a few times. It's not very big, sort of dark inside, very, very good. And Bouvert clearly knows everyone who works there.'

'Did you know he's going there tonight?' I said.

'No, but that doesn't surprise me. It's one of the few places that he won't ask me to make him a reservation at. I don't think I've ever called the restaurant for him. He just goes.'

'Did you know the Andrewses at all?' I asked. 'Did you see them ever come into the office or anything?'

'Yes, of course. Both mister and missus.'

'Would they come in often?'

'Not often, I wouldn't say, but they were important clients and treated as such. Bouvert would golf with Gerald Andrews from time to time or they'd go for dinner. Elaine Andrews and Bouvert would dine together once in a while, too.'

'Not Adamson?'

'He's not as social.'

'What else can you tell us about the nature of Gerald and Elaine Andrews' relationship with Bouvert and Adamson?'

Michelle shrugged. 'Not much. Like I said, they were important clients – they spent a lot of money at the firm.'

'Right.'

'Did you talk to the Andrewses much?' Darren said.

'Not really, no. They said hello when they came in and I booked their appointments sometimes but they'd often bypass me and call Bouvert directly on his cell, especially Gerald Andrews.'

'What's your general impression of Elaine Andrews?' said Darren.

'I'm not sure. She's beautiful, of course, and seems intelligent, but we don't talk much. She's hard to read, I guess.'

'And Gerald?'

'Rich and powerful.' She laughed. 'I don't know. Intimidating. He was handsome and nice enough to me but again I didn't have much contact with him.'

'We appreciate your help,' I said. 'Now let's get you a drink.'

Darren and Michelle and me sat drinking but Michelle didn't have much more to tell us. Darren looked tired, rough, but seemed happy to be around Michelle. He had gold sparkles underneath his eyes, embedded in the dark circles, from rubbing at his tired eyes after picking at his beer's green and gold label. I stared out on to the rainy street, thinking about the case, while Darren flirted with Michelle. The puddles were undulating and spitting in the wind and rain and changing colour with the traffic lights. A detective attempts to make sense of both what's presented to him or her and what's hidden from plain sight, modestly trying to parse things out, not accept received opinions, while maintaining one's own dignity; this is why those of us, those of us without power, are detectives, that is to say, we wake up to a world every day that has all sorts of plans for us and we spend our time figuring out said plans, battling the day, till we're too tired and need drink and/or love to put us to sleep again. This is what a detective does, I thought. Michelle had one vodka-cranberry and then left. Darren and I needed to come up with a plan.

'So what should we do?' said Darren.

'I was just thinking the same thing,' I said.

'And … ?'

'Well, we'll get there first. Stake it out.'

'We should probably pick up your gun.'

'I don't own a gun.'

'Are you serious?'

'Yes.'

'Do you have a camera?'

'Yes.'

'We should get photos of the payoff.'

'Right.'

'Also, man, we need some sort of weapon. They'll all be packing, for sure.'

'What do you suggest?'

'I don't know. What do you have?'

'A Louisville Slugger. A block of kitchen knives. You?'

'Some old golf clubs, I guess, and a baseball bat, too. We have a nail gun in the back of the boutique.'

'Great. Let's collect our gear.'

'Okay,' said Darren.

We went to my place first, since it was on the way to chez Darren and Chez Marine. Darren waited in the car out front while I ran in to get the baseball bat and camera and anything else I could find. I ran up the three small flights of stairs and dug around in my pockets for my keys. I was fumbling and flustered. While inserting my key into the lock I was greeted from behind with an X26 Taser buried in my side. I was down on the ground in a second, *neuromuscularly sedated* with 50,000 volts, and once again in cuffs. The cops had me in the back of a squad car before I knew what was happening; for a moment I thought I'd had a heart attack and/or a stroke.

23

Sitting handcuffed to a chair, I thought, *I spend an inordinate amount of time handcuffed to chairs.* They left me in the interrogation room alone for at least twenty minutes, which is pretty much SOP. Sometimes they make you wait much longer but O'Meara had a rendezvous with the Devil, I thought, or *Devils*, plural, or at least with some real bad assholes, so he couldn't waste too much time. Still, he wasn't there to attempt to intimidate me right away and left me sitting there restrained, still rattled from the 50,000 volts. On the car ride to the station one of the officers asked me if I'd ever had a taste of an X26 before and I said, 'Why would I have?' He told me that in the academy he'd volunteered to be shot up with electricity and had been OC-sprayed, too. 'Like pepper-sprayed?' I said, and he said yes and said that OC was an abbreviation for *Oleoresin Capsicum.* I asked him which was worse, the X26 or the spray, and he said they were both bad but before both they took away his service weapon and that if he'd had it after the Taser he would've shot the cadet who'd Tased him and if he'd had it after the pepper spray, he would've shot himself. 'The academy sounds like a gas,' I said, and we stopped talking for the duration of the ride.

O'Meara entered the room carrying a phonebook and we both knew what that was about. He kicked the door shut behind him and walked swiftly over to me and whacked me across the face with the book. It hurt so badly that I instantly tasted blood and felt sick.

'Okay, okay,' I said, 'I'll do whatever you want. Just don't hit me with that again. What the fuck's your problem?'

'Rick, you know damn well what's my problem.'

'Me?'

'Bingo.'

'Well, sorry I guess, but his wife hired me.'

'Yes, I know. You fell for Clytemnestra.'

'Impressive reference for a flatfoot.' O'Meara swung the phonebook back, ready to deliver another blow, but I said, 'Seriously, please don't do that again. I'm not here to fight.'

'You're here because you can't follow orders and have no respect for authority,' he said. 'But authority will simply knock you down when you get out of line. And, Rick, you're out of line.' Then, of course, he hit me across the face with the phonebook and for a second I blacked out.

'Man!' I said, sniffling, nose bloody. 'We've known each other for a long time and I get it – you're a cop and I'm a private dick and we don't like each other – but I was hired by the wife of a murdered man and now you're beating me up for doing my job.'

'Rick, you're horrible at your so-called job.'

'So be it, so you think. But you don't need to beat me like a fascist.'

'Rick, the world is fascist, first off, and secondly, you're lucky you're not dead.'

'Doesn't feel like it right now.'

'I want you to leave town.'

'Can I have till sunup since sundown's past?'

'If you don't leave town you're dead.'

'You're going to kill me?'

'Someone will. I'm doing you a favour.'

'What have you got yourself involved in?'

'Don't ask questions.'

'What the fuck's going on? Who are these people?'

'Leave town.'

'Where's Elaine?'

'I have no idea but I suspect she's far, far from here.'

'Where's Elaine?'

'I'm not lying, Rick. I have no idea.'

'What were you paid for?'

'What are you implying?'

'I'm not implying anything, O'Meara. I'm asking you straight: What did they pay you for?'

'No one's paid me for anything, Rick. I have no idea what you're talking about.'

'Cut the crap. It's time to stop playing games. I know Bouvert and Adamson have paid you for something.'

Not surprisingly, he whacked me with the phonebook again.

'Listen to me, motherfucker!' he said, dropping the phonebook and pulling my hair back and spitting on my face. 'You better shut the fuck up right now and stop asking questions or I'll kill you myself. And next time no phonebook, instead a pistol-whipping,' and he let go of my hair and pulled out his Glock from his shoulder holster, waving it in my face like a tough guy. 'I don't give a shit what you think, Rick – you don't have a clue.

I'm warning you that you need to leave town before you get yourself killed by asking too many questions.'

'So if you think someone might kill me why don't you do something about it? You're the police.'

'I am doing something about it, asshole, so don't get in my goddamn way.'

'I don't believe you.'

'I don't care. Get on a plane or bus or train and get out of town.'

'If I don't … ?'

'Leave town?'

'Yeah.'

'I thought I made that clear. You'll be killed. The only thing I could do to protect you is to lock you up. Or, you could leave town. Two choices.'

'What are you going to arrest me for?'

'I don't know. I'll stuff a bag of heroin in your shirt pocket. Whatever it takes. It's not hard.'

'I need twelve hours to solve this case.'

'All right, seriously, stop it. Enough jokes.' He put his gun away, back in its holster. 'You're deluded. You're a delusional man. Leave or I'll put you away for a long time, not just for the duration of this case. If I lock you up because you're sniffing around this case, it'll be for the rest of your life, *capisce?*'

'O'Meara – '

'Do you understand?'

'Yes. Yes, I understand.'

He uncuffed me and offered me a handkerchief for my bloodied nose.

'You'll wait here and an officer's going to escort you home, you're going to pack a bag, and then he'll see you to the train station or the airport or the bus depot, your choice – '

'Thanks.'

' – and you're going to get on your chosen mode of transportation and you're going to travel to your chosen destination and you're not going to show your face around here for a long, long time.'

'Deal.'

'I'm not really giving you a choice. Well, this or prison or death, I guess, so I am giving you a choice.'

'I'll get on a train and disappear for a while.'

'Rick, that's the first thing you've ever said I've liked.' He opened the door to the interrogation room.

'O'Meara,' I said, holding the handkerchief to my nose.

'Yeah … '

'See you in the funny pages.'

'See you in the funny pages, Rick.'

24

The same officer who shot me up with electricity drove me back to my apartment, where I was supposed to pack and then hop on a train, not to return for some time. Of course, however, I'd made my plan of escape on the car ride home. It'd stopped raining and the temperature had dropped. Officer McLaughlin was short but muscular, top heavy, with a broad chest and broad shoulders. He clearly plays rugby on weekends, I thought, and when I asked him, he was astonished, and he responded in the affirmative.

'How'd you know?' he said.

'Because I'm a detective,' I said, and unlike O'Meara he didn't make any derogatory remarks; he just seemed impressed.

I was growing to like Officer McLaughlin, despite the fact that he tased me, and I was feeling a little guilty that I was about to skip out on him, which would no doubt get him in a world of trouble and affect his career; for this, truly, I felt bad, but I had a case to solve and I wasn't about to get on a train and leave town, not yet.

When we arrived at my place, I offered Officer McLaughlin a cup of tea or coffee, having nothing else to offer, and he accepted a cup of tea, and I started to pack a bag, with some clothes and my camera, et cetera. I wanted to pack some weaponry but didn't want to look too suspicious. I told him I had to use the washroom to get cleaned up – wash away the blood – and pack my toiletry kit and he said that was fine but to be fast. I said thanks.

I ran the shower and the washroom began to fill up with steam. I washed my face quickly at the sink. I opened the small window above the shower and tried to figure out a way of hoisting myself up and out of it to the fire escape, while steam billowed and rolled out the window. The window was small, indeed, high up. I'd leave my bag behind, I decided. If I pulled myself up, I thought, I could balance on the shower-curtain bar, which was metal and very sturdy and screwed into the wall, and roll out the window. And that was exactly what I did, leaving the shower running and the washroom filling up with steam. As quietly as I could, I took the stairs down the fire escape to the street. I took back alleys to Chez Marine.

Getting to the flower shop's back entrance wasn't difficult, though I heard a police siren on the way and of course suspected it was Officer McLaughlin frantically searching for me. I slipped in the back door and didn't make a sound. I looked around at all the flowers and tools and saw a cluttered desk with, amongst other things, a glow-in-the-dark Hasbro Ouija Board with a planchette on it. It must be Julie's, I instantly thought, and then she came in to the back of the store and put her hand on her small chest, startled.

'You frightened me!' she said. 'Are you all right?'

'I'm sorry,' I said, 'but the police are after me.'

'Oh wow.'

'Is Darren around?'

'No, but I'll call his cell. I haven't seen him since you two left earlier.'

'I was with him but then I got taken away by the cops. He doesn't know. He was sitting waiting for me in the car, while I was going to grab some supplies from my place.'

'I'll call,' she said, and picked up a phone on the desk with the Ouija board. While Julie dialed, I thought I should contact Gerald Andrews with the board and ask him who stabbed him to death.

'Darren,' she said, 'I'm with Bob. At the store. He's in trouble … Okay, *bon* … *Ciao* … ' She hung up the phone.

'What's he saying?'

'He's on his way, said he just stopped at his apartment.'

'Great. *Merci, Julie.*'

'*De rien.*'

Darren was there within minutes. Of course, his first question was *what the hell happened* and I filled him in on everything: the Taser, the interrogation, the phonebook, O'Meara's Glock and splitting out the washroom window on Officer McLaughlin.

'We've only got a little over an hour till O'Meara meets up with the lawyers, so we'd better get moving,' I said.

'I'm ready,' said Darren, picking up a nail gun off a table.

'Is this is a good idea?' said Julie.

'I don't know,' I said, 'but we have to do something. I can't just sit on my hands. We have to be there for the payoff – see what this is all about, see what O'Meara's up to.'

'Do you believe he's working on the case?' said Darren. 'Like, undercover?'

'Do you?'

'No.'

'Me neither, but I've been fooled so many times that I'm open to the possibility that he's on the up and up.'

'Right … '

'We'll see, I suppose.'

'So what … ?'

'We go down to the Old Port, find this restaurant, find the pier close by, and then hide and watch. A stakeout.'

'Do you have a plan to intervene?'

'No. We'll see what goes down.'

'You two are crazy! You'll end up in prison or dead.'

'I really hope not, Julie.'

25

En route to the Old Port, I thought about what to do and didn't really have many ideas. Julie said if she didn't hear from Darren and me in a couple of hours she'd call the police.

We explained to her that the police are potentially our main problem at the moment. She seemed to understand but nevertheless said she'd contact the authorities if she hadn't heard from us in a couple of hours. Darren promised to call, at the very least, and told her to hold tight. 'We'll be okay,' he told her. I was nervous for Darren's safety, however; after all, I thought, he was a student and a flower-delivery driver who'd done me a whole host of favours, not a law enforcement officer or a criminal (when there's a difference) or a private detective – this really wasn't his problem or his case, though his help had been invaluable, I thought, even though I still wasn't sure what was going on or what was about to go down. Still, thanks to Darren, we knew about the payoff, I thought, if the payoff was still going down. Darren had brought the nail gun along and had grabbed a baseball bat and a couple of golf clubs from his apartment. Even with our armament, I thought, we were dead if things got violent, so probably best to stay out of the way, and I told Darren what I'd been thinking, emphasizing that I wanted him to stay out of harm's way, watching but not intervening, no matter what. He just nodded.

'I'm serious,' I said.

'I know.'

'It's not worth you getting hurt or killed over a bunch of rich assholes' bullshit.'

'I know.'

We drove on in silence. Darren had looked up Diavolo Cucina's address back at the boutique. He said the restaurant was right down by the water, far off from the touristy section, where you can buy fudge and watch jugglers and unicyclists and men making balloon animals, sometimes making them disappear by eating them. It was in the corner of the old city, by the waterway, near an overpass. We pulled up to the old stone building, which looked like a tiny fortress, with black steel fencing, and knew it was the restaurant, even though there wasn't a sign.

'We should wait near that little park but under the overpass,' I said, pointing to a small grassy strip across from the restaurant but before the wharf, with a few benches and picnic tables.

'I know just what to do,' said Darren, and he pulled the car up alongside a pillar under the overpass, from which we could see the restaurant's entrance, the small park and the pier. 'I've got a camera and binoculars in my knapsack.'

I turned around and unzipped the red-and-blue knapsack and took out the binoculars. I held them up to my eyes and looked over at Diavolo Cucina. It'd been a long time since I'd looked through a pair of binoculars, I thought, no longer owning a pair myself. I used to own a pair, a while back, but they got broken on a case: I'd dropped them from the rooftop of an apartment building, on a stakeout. *C'est la vie*, I thought, but it was nice to use binoculars again. I pointed them toward the wharf and the pier, where a couple of container ships were moored. I pointed them toward the park – nobody was in sight. I pointed them toward the restaurant and it seemed like the only place in the area with movement. It was dark but not too dark. The area was pretty lit up, with old-style streetlamps. They looked Victorian, I thought, but I really had no idea.

A black Mercedes pulled up to the restaurant – 'It's him,' said Darren and grabbed the camera – and lo and behold, Bouvert got out and was greeted by a valet, who took his keys and parked his car. Darren snapped photos nonstop, since his camera was digital.

He's not carrying anything, I thought.

'Okay, on schedule. What time is it?' I said.

'Twenty to ten.'

'So Bouvert probably doesn't have time to eat first.'

'Probably not, or not a whole meal. He'll probably have a drink or two first, a vodka martini, maybe.'

'Probably,' I said.

Perhaps he has the money in an envelope, I thought, tucked into a pocket of his long black overcoat. Sixty grand, however, is a lot of dough to tuck away in your coat pocket.

'Did you notice he wasn't carrying anything?' said Darren.

'I did. I was thinking maybe the money's in his coat pocket, in an envelope.'

'That's a lot of bread to keep in your pocket.'

'I agree.'

'Or maybe the money's already at the restaurant.'

'Sound thinking, Darren.'

I aimed the binoculars at the wharf, looking at the benches by the pier, looking for Michael O'Meara, but I didn't see a soul. I pointed them toward the park and thought I saw a homeless man staggering in the distance.

'No sign of Adamson,' said Darren.

'No sign of Adamson.'

'Maybe he's at the restaurant.'

'Could be. Or possibly he's sitting this one out.'

'I highly doubt that.'

'Me too.'

'Look,' said Darren, looking through the viewfinder of his camera, pointing it toward a bench on the wharf, extending the lens, zooming in on it, and applying pressure to the shutter release. On foot, O'Meara approached the bench – he looked to be alone.

'It's definitely O'Meara,' I said, pointing my binoculars in the same direction. 'Do you spot backup anywhere?'

'I don't,' said Darren, looking around.

'I think I saw a homeless guy way in the distance staggering around but I doubt he's backup.'

'So you think O'Meara's solo?'

'Hard to tell,' I said, looking around.

O'Meara sat down on the bench near the pier and lit a cigarette. Looking out on the waterway, he had his back to the restaurant. He wasn't checking his phone or making sure his gun was loaded; rather, he simply smoked his cigarette and stared out at the placid harbour water.

Despite the flower smell in the car, the area smelled of horse shit, I thought, from the tours they give of the port in horse-drawn carriages, the horses with their double bridles and blinders, and tourists in their carriages. Although I didn't see any horses or hear the clopping of their hooves on the cobblestone streets, I did smell their shit, I thought, despite the lingering smell of flowers.

There appeared to be movement. Bouvert was exiting the restaurant and I shot my binoculars over to O'Meara as his head swung around, as if he could hear Bouvert exiting the restaurant, despite the distance between them. I shot the binoculars back to Bouvert, who stood in the open doorway, which glowed softly red behind him. His frame was large, though, and blocked and absorbed most of the light.

'It's happening,' said Darren.

'Yes. Be on the lookout for any surprises.'

'I'm getting prepared right now,' said Darren, securing the nail gun beside him.

'He's got something in his hands,' I said, focusing in on Bouvert.

'What?'

'A small gym bag, it looks like … '

'So he's got the money, it's going down.'

'Looks like it.'

Bouvert crossed the street and the small park and continued toward the wharf. He was alone, I thought, by the looks of it.

'It's too bad we won't be able to hear them,' I said.

'I know. I was just thinking that, too. What can we do?'

'Not much. They'll spot us if we try and get any closer. This is a good vantage point. We just don't have any sound.'

Bouvert crossed the park and was large and probably doesn't walk much, I thought. O'Meara spotted him right away and made his way over to him. They talked. Darren took photos. They seemed to be getting along amicably, I thought, and it looked like O'Meara had made Bouvert laugh, the hearty laugh of a corpulent man. But it was hard to tell. O'Meara took the small gym bag and they shook hands. They talked a little more

and then Bouvert turned toward the restaurant and O'Meara
turned back toward the wharf.

'That went smoothly,' said Darren.

'Yeah. Something's up.'

'Clearly,' said Darren.

We watched Bouvert make his way back into the restaurant
and O'Meara walk eastward along the wharf, away from us.
O'Meara walked and strung the gym bag around his chest and
seemed carefree, from where I was sitting, with Darren in the
delivery car, watching through binoculars. Everything seemed
wrong, I thought. I felt a sense of anticipatory dread and its atten-
dant nausea. Bouvert and O'Meara were too friendly and it all
seemed too easy, I thought. I could tell Darren was thinking the
same things. I saw movement in the bushes ahead of O'Meara. A
thin man in a long black overcoat came out of the copse.

'What's going on?' said Darren.

'Someone's coming out of the park.'

Someone who looked like Adamson emerged from the park
and walked toward O'Meara. They were talking, at a distance.
The person I thought was Adamson slowly and calmly produced
a handgun from his overcoat pocket – a 9mm semi-automatic,
I thought, but it was impossible to tell from the distance – drawing a bead on O'Meara.

'Holy shit,' I said.

'Let's go!' said Darren, grabbing his nail gun and stuffing his
camera into his coat pocket.

'You stay here. Give me the gun. Take photos,' I said.

'But, Bob – '

'Don't argue. There's no time.'

I took the nail gun from Darren and got out of the hatchback
and started running toward O'Meara and who I thought was
Adamson. I was yelling. Darren was honking his car horn,

holding down on it. They were too far away. O'Meara drew his gun, but by the time he had it out he had three bullets in him. I kept running, nail gun in hand, but the person I thought was Adamson ran off. In vain, I fired off a few nails in his direction. But I had to see if O'Meara was all right, if he was alive.

O'Meara lay bleeding on the ground with his hands covered in blood resting on his bleeding chest and stomach and the small gym bag strapped across his torso. I got down beside him, propping up his head.

'Where's your phone? I'll call an ambulance.'

He didn't say a word so I searched his coat pockets and dug it out myself. 'What the fuck just happened?' I said, dialing 911. O'Meara raised his hand and smacked the phone out of mine. 'What? You want to die?'

O'Meara gave me a look and its meaning was clear. He attempted to prop himself up and began to take off the small gym bag but needed help.

'You want that off?' I said and helped him out of it.

It was clear he was going to die, as he bled in my arms. His breathing was strained because he had holes in his chest and he was gut-shot. He looked me in the eye, then at the small gym bag, then looked me in the eye again, motioning with his forehead.

'You want me to take the money,' I said.

He nodded.

'Were you working for them? Were you working for the lawyers?'

He nodded.

'Doing what?'

He just looked at me, unconcerned, moribund. He motioned at the money and then his eyes went out. I shook him, repeating his name, but nothing: O'Meara was dead. I looked around and grabbed the nail gun and grabbed the gym bag and left O'Meara's Glock and wiped my fingerprints off his cell and ran toward the hatchback. When I got close enough, I motioned for Darren to stop honking the damn horn. He did. I ran up to the car and got in.

'That's amazing,' I said. 'No one seems to have heard a thing, looks like … '

'There's no one around, except for in the restaurant, and no way they could hear gunshots from there.'

'O'Meara's dead, as I'm sure you could tell. He gave me the money, though.' I held up the gym bag, unzipping it. 'He couldn't speak but he motioned for me to take it.'

'Probably didn't want to be found dead with sixty grand.'

'That's what I figured, too, but this isn't sixty,' I said, looking at the money in the gym bag. 'It's more like twenty grand or so but mainly in twenty-dollar bills.'

'So they shortchanged him and killed him.'

'Looks like it.'

'What the fuck do we do?'

'Well, we either take the money and split or we try and take these fuckers down. They just killed a cop.'

'Bob, if they killed a cop, it's because they can.'

'So what do you propose we do?'

There was a tapping at Darren's window and I looked up and it was a 9mm doing the tapping. 'Get down,' I said, and Darren ducked and I fired off several rounds from the nail gun and the driver-side window shattered and I wasn't sure what had happened. 'Start the car but keep down.'

Darren complied. Keeping down, I looked out the shattered window and saw the man I thought was Adamson drawing a bead on us. I fired off several more rounds and heard his 9mm fall to the ground. (I think I hit him, I thought.) I got out of the car and Darren followed, brandishing a baseball bat, and I ran toward the man I thought was Adamson, who was running off. I ran up to the 9mm and picked it up with my shirtsleeve, even though I doubted there was a single usable fingerprint on the gun.

'Okay,' I said, holding up the gun, catching my breath, 'now we have the murder weapon and the loot. We probably have a photo or two, too, that turned out – at least of Bouvert paying off O'Meara.'

'Who do we go to?'

'The cops.'

'You're holding the weapon that murdered Detective Michael O'Meara.'

'But we're turning in the money,' I said.

'Bouvert and Adamson and whoever they work for, whether it's the Andrewses or whoever, are powerful people. We're not. They'll arrest you for the murder of a police detective and then you'll be killed before you stand trial.'

'So what are you saying? We should take the money and run.'

'Maybe.'

'If we confront anyone with what we've got, it should be Bouvert. I'm sure he's filling his fat face as we speak.'

26

There was no way I was letting Darren go into Diavolo Cucina, so I convinced him to wait in the car because it was integral to the plan, and in fact it *was* integral to the plan, I thought, namely, what little plan there was and there wasn't much. Regardless, I wasn't going to let him get hurt. I needed him to sit tight with the loot and the nail gun while I confronted the lawyer with the 9mm, a Browning Hi-Power (*Made In Belgium/Assembled In Portugal* embossed on its barrel), the gun that killed Detective Michael O'Meara, Robbery-Homicide. I didn't want to get my fingerprints all over it so Darren found a pair of gardening gloves in the trunk of the hatchback. I put them on.

'If I'm not out of there in ten minutes,' I said, 'I want you to call the cops.'

'But the cops'll – '

'Darren, man, they're the only option.'

'What if I hear gunfire?'

'Don't worry. I'm not going in there to get in a firefight. I'm just bringing the gun to show him what we've got. Evidence. Protection, too, but mainly evidence. If we have the gun, then he'll know we're not bullshitting about the money, and then we've got him by the balls.'

'The question remains. What if I hear gunshots?'

'Call the cops.'

'And then what?'

'We find out what the hell has been happening.'

'And then what?'

'I don't know. We turn Bouvert in.'

'It won't work.'

'We extort him. Listen, we have to do something. These people are murdering people. I can go above the heads of the corrupt people he knows in this goddamn city, if that's what has to be done. I'm a detective. With a shitload of evidence. Someone will listen. I know people too.'

'Man …'

'Yeah?'

'Be safe.'

'I've got a gun. I'll be fine.'

'I've been expecting you, Mr. James,' Bouvert said to me as I approached his table. It had a cream-coloured tablecloth and candles and was at the back of the long dark restaurant. 'Please, join me,' he said, and I sat down across from him, Bouvert with his back to a wall and me with mine to the rest of the restaurant, which was empty save for the bartender behind me at the bar and the rest of the small staff, who were in and out of the dining room, and me and Bouvert, who leaned back in his chair, a large glass of red wine in front of him, a half-emptied bottle on the table, and bread and olive oil and a plate of calamari. 'Would you like something to eat?' he said and I shook my head no. 'Some wine,' he insisted, and he picked up the bottle and poured into the glass in front of me before I could answer. 'I like the gloves. You can take them off. You won't be needing them.'

I did. And stuffed them in my coat pocket, with the gun.

'Well,' he said, forking a piece of squid into his mouth, 'say your piece.'

'I saw everything.'

'And … '

'I know you're behind everything,' I said.

He laughed. 'Believe it or not, I'm not the Evil One, Mr. James.'

'Bob's fine and you're plenty evil. I have the murder weapon in my pocket and the money stashed with an associate.'

'Okay,' he said.

'And I have photos of you paying off O'Meara, before you had him whacked.'

'*Whacked* … ?'

'I saw him shot dead in cold blood.'

'*O'Meara* … ?'

'Don't be cute.'

'Mr. James.' Bouvert pursed his lips, staring at me. 'If you leave the weapon with me and walk out that door right now, you can leave with the money and your life, if you disappear for good.'

'What happened with Elaine Andrews?'

'Still hung up on Mrs. Andrews?'

'How was she involved?'

'Mr. James, no questions. Leave me the weapon and then walk out of this restaurant.'

'Or … ?'

'Or you die.'

'You'll kill me right here?'

'If that's what needs to be done.'

'With these witnesses?'

He smiled. 'Yes.'

'For a man with such bad teeth you smile a lot, you know.'

'Also,' Bouvert said, still smiling, 'we'll kill your friend.'

'What friend?'

'The kid. Your *associate*. The delivery driver.' He took a sip of wine, swirling it around in his glass. 'The kid outside the restaurant. We'll kill him.'

I stuffed my hand in my pocket and, gloveless, grabbed the pistol and said to Bouvert, 'If you mention the kid again, I'll shoot you dead right now.' I pointed the gun toward him, still stuffed into my pocket, underneath the cream tablecloth.

'No need to get dramatic, Mr. James. I'm giving you a chance to get away, without any consequences. I'll forget about the kid completely,' he said. 'He means nothing to us. And neither do you if you disappear. Take my offer. It's the best you'll get.'

'Thank you, solicitor, but I'm interested in getting to the bottom of this case.'

'Well, you have a long way to go.'

'Then I'll keep going,' I said. 'I'll get to the truth.'

'The truth is that if you don't put that gun on the table right now and leave, then I'll send someone out to see your friend, with a large kitchen knife, and he can carve the boy up. Cut him up piece by piece. I'll get him to bring me his eyes.'

'I told you not to mention the kid,' I said, and stood up and flipped over the table. I pulled the Hi-Power out of my pocket and pointed it at Bouvert, who stood with his back up against the wall, covered in dark red wine and calamari.

The bartender behind me bent down behind the bar and popped back up with a pump-action shotgun, which he cycled as he stood. 'Drop the gun,' he said.

I could feel him pointing the gun at my back. I could feel the hole the shotgun would blast through me.

'I'll kill him,' I said. 'You drop that shotgun, barkeep.' I kept my gun levelled on Bouvert, looking straight into his truculent eyes. I think I saw beads of sweat form on his forehead.

'Protect the kid, Mr. James. Don't be an imbecile. Look at all the bodies that are piling up. I know you don't give a shit about your own life, but think of the delivery driver. You can shoot me and then you get shot and then my friend here,' he said, motioning toward the bar, 'will go outside and kill the delivery driver.'

'Who killed Gerald Andrews?'

'Does it really matter to you?'

'Yes. Who killed Gerald Andrews?'

'For argument's sake, let's say it's your friend Elaine. But in reality there were several forces that wanted Gerald Andrews dead. Is that a satisfactory answer?'

'Not at all. Why did you kill O'Meara?'

'I did no such thing,' said Bouvert.

'Let me shoot this fucking guy,' said the barkeep.

'Let's not be too hasty,' said Bouvert. 'I'm confident Mr. James will come to his senses.'

'You made a deal with the Devil, Bouvert, and one thing about the Devil – '

'Mr. James. *Ich sagte ja, dass die ganze Geschichte zum Teufel gehen wird.*'

'What does that mean?'

'I know what you're about to say, *He always comes to collect* …

'Right. You've heard that before.'

'At some point, we all make our deals. Now we find ourselves *vis à vis*. This is your turn, Mr. James. Save yourself and the boy and move on. All the people who were hurt were hurting others, et cetera, et cetera, ad nauseam. I don't think innocent people should be hurt. Save the boy. Besides, you'll walk away with twenty-five thousand dollars.'

'You'll leave the kid alone … '

'We'll forget he exists.'

'How can I trust you?'

'Do you have a choice?' Bouvert motioned for me with his hands to lower the gun. His face was now shiny with sweat. 'You have photos of me paying O'Meara. Keep them. An insurance policy, so to speak. I know I could explain them away, easily, though nevertheless they'd put you in a position where you'd be slightly more difficult to get rid of. So keep them. I'll let you be. Just disappear.'

'You'll forget about the kid.'

'What kid?' He smiled.

I lowered the gun.

'There. Good decision. Now put it on the table and be on your way,' said Bouvert.

'I'm taking the gun with me. I'll leave it outside the restaurant. I'm not walking out of here naked.'

'Fair enough.'

'And get your friend to stop pointing that shotgun at my back.'

'Put down the gun, Giancarlo.'

I walked toward the door.

'Mr. James … '

I turned around.

'You were used, but you are leaving with your life.'

'Right.'

'It's a lot more than a lot of people involved in this imbroglio can say,' said Bouvert.

27

Before returning to Chez Marine, Darren stopped at a store and picked up a six-pack. We cleaned out the glass from the car. We sat in the parking lot and drank one beer each on the hood of the car.

'What next?' said Darren.

'I'm not sure yet. But I'll leave town. Go somewhere no one knows me for a little while. But I'm leaving half the money with you.'

'Do you think it's okay, that we're taking the money?'

'I don't know what else to do with it. And I'll need something to live off while in exile. I can't go back to my place.'

'Well, you should keep all of it.'

'Man, I'd feel a lot better if I knew that some of this blood money was paying for your school. And use some of it to replace the window and fix whatever other injuries this car's sustained,' I said, smacking the hood for emphasis.

Darren took a swig of beer. 'So, we're not turning Bouvert and Adamson in?'

'No, not yet,' I said. 'I don't think we can make anything stick. Something's taking its course and we can't interfere any more than we already have or we'll be killed. At least right now. We'll keep the photos. You were right – if they can kill O'Meara with impunity, a police detective, they can kill us. Things need to cool down.'

We drove to the flower shop. Julie had waited up for us. She sat at a table, drinking red wine, and messing around with tarot cards. And I'm pretty sure Schubert's Piano Trio No. 2 in E Flat Major was playing softly in the background, though it was hard to say for certain. Darren passed me a beer and offered one to Julie, but she just held up her glass of *vin rouge*. I'd ask her to give me a reading, though I knew she'd just pull up cards xv and o, I thought, the Devil and the Fool, respectively.

'Are you two okay?' she asked.

'We're okay,' said Darren. 'No injuries sustained.'

'What happened?'

'They sh – '

'Nothing,' I said, stopping Darren. 'It was a bust.'

Julie looked at Darren and me and smiled delicately, I thought. I drank back some beer.

'I should be going home soon,' I said and yawned. 'Long night.'

'I'll give you a lift,' said Darren.

'Thanks, man.'

'I can drop you off first, Julie.'

'Thanks.'

'Okay,' said Darren to Julie. '*Allons-y, allons-o.*'

Julie didn't live too far from the shop, and of course I wasn't going home. For all intents and purposes, I thought, I didn't have a home. I'd decided I'd go east. I'd go to the coast and lie low for a while. I'd work on my case notes. I'd get some badly needed rest. I'd escape suffocating, soul-sucking people, I thought, for a while at least. We pulled up to Julie's walkup, with its black iron spiral staircase and small garden out front.

'Nice to meet you, Bob,' said Julie, and I turned around and looked in the back seat and she was smiling. 'See you soon.'

'*À bientôt*,' I said (I hope, I thought).

'*À bientôt, Bob*,' she said and leaned in and kissed both my cheeks lightly. 'Bye.'

'Bye,' we said.

'Do you want another drink for the road?' said Darren.

'What are you thinking?'

'Chez Carlos … '

'I really should be hittin' the trail.'

'What about the bar in the train station?'

'Naw. That place is dead trousers. Just drop me at the metro up here. It's dangerous for you to be seen with me right now.'

'Am I gonna hear from you?'

'Yes. Soon. I'll write, or call. I've got your card.'

'Bob, man, thanks for everything,' said Darren.

We pulled up to the metro stop. 'There's a little over twelve grand in the glovebox. Don't forget to pay for any damages to the car. Be well, comrade, and thank you for all your help. You're a good detective, Darren.'

'Thank you. But no one's getting punished and you have to skip town. I mean, as far as the case goes, we failed.'

'Well, yes, probably,' I said. 'But we know more about it than we did in the beginning, I think.'

'Maybe.'

'I'll be in touch and make sure everything's jake.'

'Good. Farewell, Bob.'

'Talk soon.'

'*Leb wohl.*'

28

I took the escalator down into the metro and grabbed a newspaper and a pack of gum and a bottle of water at the newsstand. When I got on the train to the station, I flipped through the paper (*The Examiner*, i.e., the local rag) looking for anything on the case. I found an article saying that the police suspected a *drug addict* of breaking into the Andrewses' and stabbing Gerald Andrews to death. They had an unnamed suspect in custody, I read. He had priors. The article also said that the murderer stole *antique jewellery* from the Andrewses. Tomorrow's paper will say that O'Meara was killed by a *crazed vagrant*, I thought. We pulled into the station and I left my newspaper on the seat for whoever wanted to read that bullshit and I took an escalator to the station's main floor and I went to the ticket counter and bought a ticket to a small coastal town. There was a night train, so I didn't have to wait long, and I drank a large bottle of water while waiting, which wasn't long, as I said. The train ride was nice, relaxing, even, as I watched the fields with cattle and crops go by and lightning flash in the distance and the cows were clearly agitated. I thought of O'Meara lying on the ground, ventilated, with blood globules all over his hands and more blood gushing out of his chest and stomach. I thought about Bouvert, with wine and food on his clothes and his back to the wall while I held him there at gunpoint. I thought about Elaine – about how I fell for her and about how she'd deceived me and about how she'd disappeared. At least she was alive, I thought, if in fact she was alive, which I suspected she was. She considers me a sad sap, I thought, and a crummy detective, if she considers me at all, which she most likely doesn't. I was merely a stepping stone, I thought, an incidental player – and this was incontrovertible fact. I drank two miniature bottles of Johnnie Walker. I even slept dreamlessly for a couple of hours. Around five-thirty in the a.m., the train pulled into the station and the only luggage I had on me was the small gym bag full of cash: about twelve grand or a little more. I'd have to go in to town and buy clothes and toiletries, I thought, but that would have to wait. It was late – or early, rather – but there were taxis out front of the station. It was still dark out and cold. I got in a taxi and said, 'Une auberge, s'il vous plaît.' No one knows me here, I thought, and it felt incredible – anonymity's unburdening power was unexpected and welcomed. I'd live quietly, I thought, try to go unnoticed. I got a room at a small inn with an ocean view and went upstairs and collapsed on the bed. I was exhausted, of course, but still rattled, a little wired. I fell asleep briefly, for a few minutes maybe, dreaming of I'm not sure what, but woke with a hypnic jerk. I stood up and walked over to the window, which looked out onto the sea. Waves smashed up against a giant rock formation, slowly and insistently eroding the peninsula. The sky was dark and over-cast. And the ocean looked like billions of tons of shimmering mercury, rising and falling, lit greyly by the dim moon.

The author would like to thank the following:

A. Carless, K. Hutchinson, M. Iossel, E. Munday, L. Nash, J. Novakovich, P. Powell, A. Szymanski, C. Tucker, H. Waechtler, E. Walsh and (esp.) A. Wilcox. And his friends and family, &c.

John Goldbach is the author of *Selected Blackouts*, a collection of stories. He lives in Montreal.

Typeset in Albertina and Albertus.

Printed at the old Coach House on bpNichol Lane in Toronto,
Ontario, on Zephyr Antique Laid paper, which was manufac-
tured, acid-free, in Saint-Jérôme, Quebec, from second-growth
forests. This book was printed with vegetable-based ink on a
1965 Heidelberg KORD offset litho press. Its pages were folded
on a Baumfolder, gathered by hand, bound on a Sulby Auto-
Minabinda and trimmed on a Polar single-knife cutter.

Edited and designed by Alana Wilcox
Cover by Chris Tucker
Author photo by Kate Hutchinson

Coach House Books
80 bpNichol Lane
Toronto ON M5S 3J4
Canada

416 979 2217
800 367 6360

mail@chbooks.com
www.chbooks.com